D0475797

Nicobobinus

Terry Jones

NICOBOBINUS

illustrated by
Michael Foreman

For Elizabeth Gardner

First published in Great Britain 1985 by
Pavilion Books Limited
196 Shaftesbury Avenue, London WC2H 8JL
in association with Michael Joseph Limited
44 Bedford Square, London WC1B 3DP

Designed by Lawrence Edwards

British Library Cataloguing in Publication Data

Jones, Terry
Nicobobinus.
I. Title II. Foreman, Michael, 1938-
823'.914[J] PZ7

ISBN 1-85145-000-9

Printed and bound in Italy by
Arnoldo Mondadori Editore

Contents

Continues overleaf

I

How Nicobobinus Didn't Weed His Doorstep

This is the story of the most extraordinary child who ever stuck his tongue out at the Prime Minister. His name was Nicobobinus. He lived a long time ago, in a city called Venice, and he could do anything.

Of course, not everybody knew he could do anything. In fact, only his best friend, Rosie, knew he could, and nobody took any notice of anything Rosie said, because she was always having wild ideas anyway.

One day, for example, Rosie said to Nicobobinus: 'Let's pull up every single weed on your doorstep.'

'Let's not,' said Nicobobinus (which is what Rosie thought he would say).

'In that case,' replied Rosie, 'let's discover the Land of Dragons!'

'Don't be daft!' said Nicobobinus. 'How can we do that?'

'Because *you* can do anything,' said Rosie.

So, the next morning, just as it was getting light, Rosie threw little pebbles up at Nicobobinus's shutters. Nicobobinus was still half asleep when he looked out.

'What's the matter, Rosie?' he asked.

'Ssh!' whispered Rosie. 'I've got the buns and the lemonade.'

'What for?' asked Nicobobinus.

'Supplies for the road!' whispered Rosie.

'Where are you going?' asked Nicobobinus.

'We're going to find the Land of Dragons,' whispered Rosie. 'Don't you remember?'

'Oh . . . I thought you might have forgotten about that,' said Nicobobinus.

'No fear!' said Rosie. 'It's one of the best ideas you've ever had!'

'Is it?' said Nicobobinus.

'Yes!' said Rosie.

'What about the weeding?' said Nicobobinus.

'Come on!' said Rosie.

So they set off through the early morning town. When they got to the end of the narrow street where they lived, they met a Nightwatchman who said: 'Where are you two going at this hour?'

'We're going to look for the Land of Dragons,' said Nicobobinus.

'You can't do that at this time of the morning,' said the Nightwatchman.

'Oh yes he can!' said Rosie. 'He can do anything.'

'Not during curfew!' said the Nightwatchman. But before he could grab them, Rosie and Nicobobinus were sprinting away as fast as they could.

And they didn't stop running until they had crossed three bridges, and tripped over a dog that was lying asleep under a garden wall. Rosie's bottle of lemonade smashed against the wall, and the dog leapt to its feet, barking as if it

had thought Dogs' Doomsday had arrived. For a moment, they were sure it was going to bite them, but then it noticed the two buns that had rolled into the gutter, and it wolfed them down, barked 'Thank you!' and ran off to tell its friends.

'We're not going to get very far without supplies,' said Rosie gloomily.

'I wonder if I could pick a few of those?' said Nicobobinus, gazing up at an apple-tree on the other side of the garden wall.

'Of course you can!' said Rosie. 'Stand on my shoulders.'

So Nicobobinus stood on Rosie's shoulders, and climbed onto the wall. But the tree was further away than he thought, and as he reached out, he lost his balance, and fell with a crash, down into the most magnificent garden he had ever been in.

Nicobobinus looked back up at the high wall, but there was no way he could climb back.

'What am I going to do?' he yelled.

'You'll think of something!' Rosie yelled back, crossing her fingers *very* hard.

'Oy!' said a voice behind Nicobobinus.

Nicobobinus didn't stop to look who it was – he ran . . . straight into a tree.

'Got you!' said the voice, and Nicobobinus felt five thick fingers on his neck.

'Ow!' said Nicobobinus.

'I've been waiting for you,' said the voice, and Nicobobinus felt five more thick fingers round his wrist. But Nicobobinus did his old trick. Instead of trying to run away (which is, I think, what I might have done) he doubled himself up and went backwards as fast as he could, so the man's legs were knocked from under him, and he tumbled head-first over Nicobobinus and landed in a pile of leaves.

'Are you all right?' called Rosie, but she didn't hear any reply, except for the man, who growled:

'Just you wait . . . Both of you!'

'Oh dear,' said Rosie. 'Sounds like trouble. . . .'

And she was right.

2

What Happened on the Other Side of the Wall

Nicobobinus didn't stop to think. He just ran as fast as he could, across the lawn, down the path, round a hedge and into a little shed, and bolted the door.

'Open up!' cried the Man, and the hinges creaked and the door shook, as he banged it with his fists.

'That door's not going to last long,' thought Nicobobinus to himself, and he dragged a large, old stone roller up against it.

'Open this door at once, d'you hear?' the Man was shouting. But Nicobobinus didn't hear him. In fact, he didn't hear anything at all – he was too amazed by what he had found.

'You'll have to come out eventually,' the Man was saying, 'and the longer you leave it, the worse it'll be for you.'

But he could have saved his breath. Nicobobinus wasn't listening. He was on his knees examining what he had revealed when he moved the roller. He brushed off the dust, and undid the catch, and then lifted it up. . . .

'Right! I'm going to break this door down!' said the

Man. And then, because he knew he'd have to repair the door himself, he added: 'Do you hear?'

But Nicobobinus didn't hear. Nicobobinus wasn't there. He had disappeared through the trap-door he had discovered, and was running down stone steps that were slippery with slime and that smelt of graveyards, and that went down and down, deeper and deeper into the ground, until it became pitch black.

'Rosie,' said Nicobobinus to himself, 'this is all *your* fault!'

He heard his heart pounding, and he heard his steps echoing along the dank rock of the narrow passageway, that went down and down, until all at once there was nothing, and before he realised he was falling in the blackness . . . he was!

Several thoughts flashed through his mind at the same time, in the way that thoughts can. The first was something on the lines of: 'Bother!' (only a bit ruder). The second was a rather unkind thought about his best friend, who had instigated the whole expedition, and it involved her dangling over a snake pit, while numerous fierce dragons flew at her chanting: 'How could you do it to him? Poor Nicobobinus!' The third thought was: 'Suppose it's a well? A deep, unused well, with slimy, slippery sides that you could never climb, and icy water at the bottom that . . .'

At this point, he discovered it was not a well . . . He made this discovery very suddenly, and very painfully.

'Ouff!' said Nicobobinus, and he lay there in the pitch blackness, with not a single breath left in his body, for what seemed like the whole winter, but was probably only a few seconds.

He came to himself, in fact, just as a stone hit him on the head.

'Ouff!' said Nicobobinus again, and then realised he could hear footsteps high above him.

'Stop sir!' he called out. But the footsteps kept on coming down.

'Ah ha! I've got you now!' said a voice, alarmingly high above him.

'Oh no, sir! You don't understand, sir!' said Nicobobinus 'You mustn't come any further, there's a . . .'

'I've got you!' cried the Man. 'And I shall beat every bone in your body, until it is black and . . .'

Nicobobinus supposed the man was going to say 'blue', but, in fact, the next word he uttered sounded more like: 'Bkfahooharrrrrgggghhhhgmph!' It was not a word with which Nicobobinus was at all familiar, but he understood its meaning perfectly, and moved smartly out of the way.

Crash.

'Are you all right!' he asked.

There was silence.

Nicobobinus felt his way back in the pitch dark, until his hand touched the Man's leather jerkin. The Man was lying still as death, but he *was* breathing.

'I must get help', said Nicobobinus to himself, and he began groping around in the blackness to find another way out. When he found it, however, his heart sank. The only exit appeared to be a narrow gap, down by the floor, no more than a foot high.

'I can't squirm through *that* in the pitch dark!' he said to himself, but at that very moment, he heard Rosie's cheerful voice behind him saying: 'You can do it!'

Nicobobinus span round, and there – to his immense surprise – was ... nothing. Just blackness ... No Rosie ... No anybody ...

'But I don't know if it leads anywhere!' he said to the voice in his head. 'And it's such a tight squeeze – I might get stuck!'

He didn't hear Rosie's voice again, but he knew what it would have said, and that was how he found himself wriggling down a narrow passage of stone in the pitch black.

He squirmed and he wriggled there in the black for a long, long time, and the tunnel didn't get any wider. It got narrower, until he could hardly inch along it.

'I'm going back!' he said to himself, but he didn't. He just kept wriggling and squirming, wriggling and squirming, until suddenly he found he could stand up. He took a pace forward, and immediately fell over some steps leading up.

'Ow!' he said, although what he really meant was: 'Thank goodness!'

He began to climb, and he was still climbing some minutes later, round and round, up and up. 'It must be a tower,' he thought, 'or the grandest house in Venice!' But at that very moment, he saw a crack of light in front of him. He stretched out his hand and found himself touching a catch, that clicked softly in the dark. A panel suddenly slid open, and Nicobobinus stepped through into the most amazing room he'd ever seen.

3

The Golden Man

Everything in the room seemed to be made of gold, and in the centre was a huge four-poster bed, covered with golden silk.

But before Nicobobinus had time to so much as lift a finger to touch anything, he heard a heavy tread outside the door, and he saw the handle turning and the door slowly start to open.

Without thinking twice, Nicobobinus dived under the bed, and lay there with his heart beating. He heard hard, heavy feet stamping into the room.

'What's this?' said a hard, heavy voice, and Nicobobinus just couldn't stop himself peering out from under the bed. There stood a man who was made of gold. He had golden shoes and golden stockings. His breeches and jerkin were made of cloth of gold, and he wore a hat of pure gold leaf.

'There's someone here!' cried the man, and his yellow face turned red for a moment. 'Somebody in my house!' he cried. 'Somebody in my ROOM!' And the golden chandelier

rattled, and the golden candlesticks upon the golden table knocked together.

Then the Golden Man turned a golden key in the golden lock of the door, and began to look around.

'I've been in tighter spots', said Nicobobinus to himself, although he didn't really think so. And then he thought: 'But wait a moment! I can't *hide* – I've come to get help!' So, while the Golden Man was looking in a big golden chest at the other end of the room, Nicobobinus climbed out from under the bed, and stood there, and said: 'I've come to get help!'

The Golden Man leapt in the air, twizzled around and cried out: 'Robber! Thief!'

'I'm not a robber,' said Nicobobinus.

'Yes you are!' cried the Golden Man, 'You're dressed in rags!'

'These aren't rags!' exclaimed Nicobobinus, who had put on his best clothes for the expedition.

'You're after my gold!' screamed the Golden Man.

'No I'm not!' said Nicobobinus.

'Everybody is!' cried the Golden Man. 'And look at you! Not a scrap of gold on your body!'

'I've come to get help!' said Nicobobinus.

'To carry off my gold!' screamed the Golden Man.

'No!' shouted Nicobobinus. 'To rescue an injured man down there!' And he pointed to the secret stairs up which he had come. Now perhaps the Golden Man had not noticed the open panel before, for when he saw it, he turned first red, then blue, and then he raced across to the panel, slammed it shut, and stood there trembling with rage and glaring at Nicobobinus.

'Don't you understand?' shouted Nicobobinus, running up to him, and shaking him by his golden shoulders. 'He needs help! You've got to hurry!'

'*I'll* give you gold,' said the Golden Man with a smile that somehow made Nicobobinus go cold inside. And he took one of Nicobobinus's hands off his shoulder, and held it in his own golden hand, and he squeezed ... and he squeezed. ...

Nicobobinus went even colder inside, and he felt the most curious sensation. It was like the bath must feel as the water is running out down the plughole. Nicobobinus felt the life running out of his body – down his arm and out through his hand. And his hand went numb, as the Golden Man squeezed ... and squeezed ... and ... Nicobobinus felt his head swimming ... he felt a darkness at the back of his skull, coming down as the Golden Man squeezed ... and squeezed ... and Nicobobinus knew he had to get free ... But the darkness was now touching his brain ... and his body would not obey him ... and the Golden Man squeezed ... and squeezed ... and suddenly Nicobobinus wrenched his hand free, and sprang back!

'That's only a little gold,' grinned the Golden Man. 'Don't you want more? *Lots* more?'

Nicobobinus looked down at his hand that now hung numb and useless by his side, and he gaped. He couldn't believe his eyes. He touched his hand, and he tried in vain to move the fingers, but it was no use. His hand had turned to pure, cold gold.

'Just think!' said the Golden Man. 'You could have a golden arm, and a golden neck, and a golden chest, and golden ...'

'You'll not turn *me* into gold for your coffers!' shouted Nicobobinus, and he turned and ran to the door, but, of course, it was still locked, and before he could unlock it, he felt the cold fingers of the Golden Man around his neck, squeezing ... and squeezing ... and he felt the blackness

descending . . . but he did his old trick again, and ran backwards as fast as he could, and the Golden Man fell to the floor with a clatter and clank. Nicobobinus leapt over him, but as he did the Golden Man grabbed his foot.

Before Nicobobinus could say 'Ouch!' or 'Ouff!' or anything interesting like that, he felt the Golden Man squeezing . . . and squeezing . . . his foot . . . and then he discovered he couldn't look round at the Golden Man, because the back of his neck seemed to be solid and stiff, and he knew that the skin on his neck had been turned to pure, cold gold too.

'What's the matter?' grinned the Golden Man. 'I thought you liked gold?' And he held onto Nicobobinus's foot, and he squeezed . . . and he squeezed . . .

'I prefer football!' cried Nicobobinus, and he kicked as hard as he could with his free foot, and the Golden Man yelled, and clutched his head, and Nicobobinus shot under the bed again, dragging his golden foot after him.

'He'll turn me all to gold!' thought Nicobobinus. 'And *then* what'll Rosie do?' But he didn't have time to think any more about that, because the Golden Man's fingers were suddenly touching his nose!

'Uh-oh!' cried Nicobobinus, and pulled back as he saw the Golden Man peering under the bed at him.

'*Everybody* likes gold!' grinned the Golden Man. 'Here's a golden nose for you!' and he dived under the bed with surprising speed. But Nicobobinus was even faster – he had rolled out from the other side, and was shinning up one of the bedposts (as fast as he could with a golden hand and a golden foot) before the Golden Man could get at him.

'Don't you want to have the pair!' cried the Golden Man, and he grabbed Nicobobinus's other foot, as he tried to pull himself up onto the canopy above the bed. The

Golden Man began squeezing ... and squeezing ... and pulling him down, and Nicobobinus felt the life ebbing away down his foot, and he knew that if he didn't do something at once, he would soon be just another lump of gold in the Golden Man's coffers. But there was neither handhold nor fingerhold on the canopy above the bed, and the Golden Man seemed to be growing stronger and stronger, as he squeezed ... and he squeezed ... and Nicobobinus felt his foot and his ankle turning to gold, and do what he might he just hadn't the strength to pull himself up out of reach.

So he did something so obvious that I don't think I would ever have thought of it – even if you would. He *let go*! And the moment he let go, he shot down suddenly onto the Golden Man's shoulders. In his surprise, the Golden Man let go of Nicobobinus's foot, and then Nicobobinus clamped his legs around the Golden Man's neck, and put his good hand over the Golden Man's eyes.

'Hey!' cried the Golden Man, and he started blundering

blindly around the room, trying to shake Nicobobinus off his back. But Nicobobinus hung on tight.

First they banged into a bedpost. 'Ow!' cried the Golden Man. Then they banged into the door. 'Ouf!' he cried. And then they turned right around, and headed for the window.

At that moment, there was a hammering on the door.

'Are you all right, your Lordship?' cried the servants. 'Why are you shouting?'

'Help!' cried the Golden Man. 'Heeeeeeeeeeeeeeelp!'

This was the moment when Nicobobinus took his hand away from the Golden Man's eyes, so that the Golden Man just had time to see the beautiful patterns on the stained-glass window, before he crashed head-first through it. He clawed the air for a moment, and then plummetted down into the Grand Canal.

And Nicobobinus followed after him ...

4

How Nicobobinus Must Have Got Very, Very Smelly

The Grand Canal is a fine sight, but Nicobobinus didn't really appreciate the splendid view he had of it, as he hurtled after the Golden Man – even though he could see right down as far as the Rialto Bridge (which in those days was made entirely of wood). What he *did* appreciate, however, was the sight of a bracket sticking out of the wall, which he seized with his good hand as he went through the window. Unfortunately it came away with his weight, but it did slow him down enough to enable him to grab the window ledge as he began to plummet. And now, there he was, dangling a hundred feet above the Grand Canal, with one golden hand and two golden feet, wondering how on earth he was ever going to pull himself back again.

'I don't care if I never see another piece of gold as long as I live!' said Nicobobinus to himself. 'Which probably won't be very long!' he added.

But I think he was lucky in one respect: because of his stiff golden neck, he couldn't look down and see the dizzy drop below him – nor could he see the wreckage of the gondola that the Golden Man had smashed in half as he fell. Instead, Nicobobinus fixed his eyes on the window, and said: 'I can't do it!'

Then he thought of what he would say to Rosie, if ever he saw her again, and this cheered him up so much that he suddenly found himself heaving his body up over the window ledge, and collapsing in a heap, back in the Golden Man's room. At that moment, however, the door burst open, and three servants rushed in.

'Murderer! Thief! Where is His Lordship?' they cried.

'He's gone for a swim,' said Nicobobinus, and nodded towards the broken window.

Their jaws dropped in unison, so you'd have sworn they were about to sing a song, and then they dashed to the window, like a man with six legs.

Nicobobinus didn't wait to hear what they thought about the view, even though the sun was now just catching the Rialto Bridge in its first rays, and you or I might have thought it was worth painting a picture of it.

Nicobobinus had gone, and the door had slammed, and been locked again from the outside, before the servants had time to so much as spin round and shout: 'Hey!' – which, under the circumstances, seemed rather a pointless thing to shout anyway.

But Nicobobinus didn't even hear it. He was sprinting down the corridor as fast as his golden feet would carry him.

Half the people in the house were rushing upstairs, and half were rushing downstairs, but everyone was in such a state they didn't take the slightest notice of Nicobobinus. And Nicobobinus kept his head down, which is why he bumped head-on into a chamber-maid, who was carrying a chamber-pot out of one of the bedrooms. The pot smashed on the beautiful tiled floor, and the contents sprayed all over the corridor, and Nicobobinus slid onto his bottom in the middle of it, and said: 'Good Heavens! Rosie!'

'Follow me!' said the chamber-maid (who was, indeed, Rosie) and the two of them ran back through the bedroom, and down a back staircase. And they didn't stop running until they got to a door that led out of the Golden Man's house onto a narrow back street.

'I found this door open, so I slipped in, and pretended to be a chamber-maid,' explained Rosie.

'Well, you were the best chamber-maid I've ever run into!' said Nicobobinus.

'But what's happened to your hand?' cried Rosie. 'And your feet?'

'Tell you later,' said Nicobobinus. 'Come on!'

'Where are we going?' asked Rosie, but Nicobobinus was away.

Rosie followed him round the corner, until they came to the Golden Man's garden wall, where it had all begun.

'Over we go!' said Nicobobinus.

Rosie gaped at him. 'What?!' she said. 'You're not going back!'

But Nicobobinus had climbed onto Rosie's shoulders and was hauling her up onto the wall, even as she spoke.

'There's a man badly injured in there,' said Nicobobinus, pointing at the shed beyond the hedges.

'But we've only just escaped!' cried Rosie.

'If we don't help him he'll die,' replied Nicobobinus.

'You're crackers!' said Rosie.

'We're going to need a light, a blanket and some rope,' said Nicobobinus.

'I'll get them,' said Rosie, and she did.

5

How Nicobobinus and Rosie Did a Very Good Thing, and the Reward They Got For It

With a flickering candle in his good hand, and the rope over his shoulder, Nicobobinus ventured once again down the slippery stone steps. When he reached the point where the stone steps stopped abruptly, he found himself looking down into a gloomy pit, at the bottom of which he could just make out the crumpled figure of a man, who groaned when he saw the light, and whispered: 'Help . . .'

It took Rosie and Nicobobinus a long time to make a stretcher out of the blanket, tie the man in, and haul him back up again, especially since Nicobobinus had only one hand that was much use. While they worked, Nicobobinus told Rosie about his adventures inside.

'Wow!' said Rosie. 'You must be worth a lot of money now.'

'Pull!' said Nicobobinus, and they heaved the man up a few more inches.

'We'd better watch out you don't get stolen!' said Rosie.

'We'd better find out how to change me back!' said Nicobobinus, and they gave a final heave, and pulled the man up beside them.

The man looked at Nicobobinus, and then he looked at Rosie, and then he looked at Nicobobinus again, and then he said: 'Ah ha! Caught you at last!'

'Don't be daft!' replied Rosie. 'He's just rescued you!'

'You're badly injured,' said Nicobobinus.

'That's true,' said the man, looking down at his legs.

They carried the man up the slippery steps as well as they could, but they kept having to rest because he was very heavy, and Nicobobinus and Rosie were only quite small.

When they got into the open air, they laid him in the blanket gently on the ground.

'Don't bother to say thank you,' said Rosie. And the man didn't. He was staring at Nicobobinus's hand.

'Maybe you saved my life,' said the man, 'so maybe I'll do you a favour.'

'That's very kind of you,' said Nicobobinus.

Then the man lowered his voice, and whispered two words. He said them so quietly and so quickly that Rosie didn't hear them at all, and Nicobobinus said: 'Pardon?' But the man wouldn't repeat them. He just said: 'That's the only thing that'll cure you!' and then looked very hunted and whispered: 'And now get out of here!'

'Charming!' said Rosie.

'Help! Thieves!' shouted the man. 'Robbers in the garden! They've broken my legs!'

'Of all the ungrateful creeps!' exclaimed Rosie.

'Let's get out of here!' said Nicobobinus, and they did.

'Intruders!' yelled the man, as Nicobobinus and Rosie ran for the wall.

'Help! I've been attacked!' he screamed, as Nicobobinus climbed onto Rosie's shoulders.

'Stop!' cried a soldier who suddenly appeared from the house with a crossbow.

'Hurry!' yelled Rosie, as Nicobobinus hauled her up the wall.

'Look out!' cried Nicobobinus, as an arrow thudded into the brickwork, just missing Rosie's foot.

'Get them!' yelled the soldier.

'Phew!' said Nicobobinus, as they dropped down to the ground on the other side.

'Come on!' cried Rosie, and they sprinted off, with Nicobobinus's golden feet ringing down the endless narrow streets and alleys and canal ways.

When they finally slumped down together in the shelter of a doorway, Nicobobinus looked at Rosie and grinned.

'What have you got to grin about?' asked Rosie.

'Well,' said Nicobobinus, 'you said I could do it . . . and I did!' And he pulled two apples out of his jerkin.

'You didn't pick those when we were escaping just now, did you?' exclaimed Rosie.

'Er no,' replied Nicobobinus, 'I'm afraid they're windfalls.'

'Well, you're a cool customer, I must say!' said Rosie, and bit into her apple. 'Now tell me what the man said to you.'

'He said he'd do me a favour,' said Nicobobinus.

'But what did he *whisper*?' asked Rosie.

'Well . . .' replied Nicobobinus, 'I'm not quite sure I heard it right . . .'

'What did it sound like?' asked Rosie.

'Well . . .' said Nicobobinus, looking a bit embarrassed, 'I'm not absolutely sure I heard it right, but I *think* he said the only thing that'll cure me is . . .'

'Yes?' said Rosie, who hated suspense.

'Dragon's blood!' said Nicobobinus.

Rosie was just about to say: 'Then we're going to the right place!' but she didn't, because she suddenly found herself gazing up into the faces of four of the most evil-looking men she'd ever seen in her life.

6

How Nicobobinus Was Kidnapped

''Ello!' said a man with a ring in his nose, 'That looks like solid gold to me!'

'Ow!' said Nicobobinus, as one of them tapped his golden foot with a knife.

'It is!' said the man with the knife. 'And look at his hand and his neck as well! He must be worth a fortune!'

'Put him in the sack,' said the man with the ring in his nose.

'Good idea!' said the small man behind him.

'Shut up!' said the man with the ring in his nose.

'Yes, Captain, anything you say, Captain!' said the small man, who was then hit rather hard on the back of his head by the ugliest of the three.

'Wait a minute!' I can hear you saying. 'You said there were *four* of these men.'

Well, I admit I did ... but, you see, one of them (the man with the knife, in fact) had suddenly vanished into thin air ... just like that! His disappearance was simply one of those many unrecorded mysteries of which our life is full. I wish I could be more informative about what actually happened to him, but the truth is: I simply do *not* know.

The man who vanished was called Basilcat, and he had never been exactly popular. The Captain never mentioned Basilcat's disappearance, because he preferred the crew to think that he knew everything that went on, and - what is more - controlled it. The crew, for their part, never referred to Basilcat again, because they assumed that he must have incurred the wrath of the Captain (who knew everything and controlled everything) and that the Captain must somehow or other have had him removed. And they feared the same fate might befall them, if they asked questions. Therefore they remained totally silent about Basilcat's extraordinary disappearance.

As for Nicobobinus and Rosie, they were simply unsure as to whether it was three or four desperadoes who bundled Nicobobinus into a sack, carried him down to a waiting skiff, and headed off for where the tall ships were moored.

Rosie watched him go, and said to herself: 'Great! Just what we wanted!' As I say, people often thought Rosie's ideas were a bit wild.

But Rosie didn't think twice. She jumped down into a little empty boat, that was lying nearby, and rowed after the skiff as fast as she could. Even Rosie's fastest, however, was no match for the men who had kidnapped Nicobobinus, and she soon lost them among the forest of masts of the lighters and the gondolas, the dinghies, schooners, caravelles, galleons, brigs, riggers, frigates and fishing smacks.

And all the time, Rosie found herself wondering what those desperate men might do to Nicobobinus. 'Well, I suppose the best they might do is sell him as a job lot,' she said to herself. 'But the worst . . . and most likely . . . is that . . . they'll . . .' she could hardly bring herself to say it. 'They'll . . . cut . . . his feet off . . . and his hand off . . . and . . . and . . . his neck . . . and . . . oh! Poor Nicobobinus! And it's all my fault!' And she rowed and searched until night fell, muttering: 'I wonder where the Land of Dragons *is*?'

7

The Extraordinary Story of Something Rosie Did

Rosie shivered in the moonlight, and tied her boat alongside the quay. She was just about to climb out, when she heard footsteps on the paving stones, and a man's voice whispered: 'From the *Santa Margharita*?'

Rosie just kept her head down, and did not reply. The man withdrew back into the shadow, and all was silent again. Rosie was lying in her boat, wondering what to do, when she heard the plash of an oar, and another small boat appeared, with a man standing at the back, rowing in the Venetian manner. He gave a low whistle, and once more, the man on the quay stepped out into the moonlight, and murmured: '*Santa Margharita*?'

'Dr Sebastian?' asked the man in the boat.

Evidently the doctor nodded, for without any more words he handed over the bag he was carrying, and climbed down into the boat himself, and the oarsman steered them away into the darkness.

I don't know how Rosie knew, nor could she explain it afterwards, when she was telling Nicobobinus the story, but the fact is that it flashed into Rosie's mind that she ought to follow these two men.

'What are they doing – sneaking around at this time of night anyway?' she said to herself, as she struggled after them. 'It's long past curfew!'

Fortunately it was not long before they pulled up in the lee of one of the great trading carracks, moored in the harbour, and the sailor gave another low whistle.

A rope ladder dropped softly over the side of the ship, and the two men climbed silently up, accompanied only by the clanking of whatever the doctor carried in his bag.

They seemed in quite a hurry, and disappeared from Rosie's view, leaving the rope ladder hanging. Before she had time to wonder whether it was a good idea or not, Rosie found herself up the ladder and on board the deck of the carrack.

A torch was burning in a bracket on the poop-deck wall, and next to it was a small window. Rosie crept across the deck, and cautiously peered in. The sight that met her eyes made her feel relieved and horrified all at the same time. She was relieved because there was Nicobobinus still alive and kicking – or at least he was *trying* to kick, and the reason why he *couldn't* kick was what filled Rosie with such horror.

Nicobobinus was stark naked, and he was tied down on the Captain's table, and the doctor had just opened his bag, and was arranging the contents on the table beside Nicobobinus. There were scissors of various sizes, several sharp scalpels, two saws and ... Rosie didn't want to see any more! She ducked down, and looked desperately around the ship. She tried not to say to herself: 'They're going to cut him up – *alive*!' But she couldn't help it, and she kept repeating it to herself, as she cast her eyes around frantically searching for a way to save him. 'I've got to hurry!' she said, and then added for the fourteenth time: 'They're going to cut him up – *alive*!' and then kicked herself for saying it.

Rosie stole another glance through the poop-deck window. The Doctor had rolled his sleeves up, and had raised his biggest saw. The Captain was pointing to Nicobobinus's foot. Rosie gasped: 'They're going to ... to ... to ... *do* it!' And she turned around, and then she did what you may think was a rather an odd thing. She smiled.

As I say, Rosie was always having wild ideas, and, as you can probably guess, she'd just had another one. There wasn't time to work out whether it was a good idea or a bad idea. It was the only idea she had, and she just did it. She seized the torch that was still guttering and spluttering beside the window, ran across the deck, and hurled it into the cargo. Then she ran back to the Captain's cabin, flung the door open, and yelled (in as deep a voice as she could) 'Fire!'

Rosie was amazed at just how effective her plan was. She had expected a reaction, but she hadn't expected it to be so instantaneous. At the word 'Fire!' every single man in the room - except for the Doctor and Nicobobinus - went white as a sheet, and stampeded for the door. Not one of them stopped to ask Rosie who she was, and not one of them stopped to ask how it had happened. They didn't even go: 'Fire?' or 'Gosh!' or 'Do you think we should put it out?' They just ran like men possessed by every devil in hell, across the deck to where several bales of straw were by now blazing away merrily. They stopped for a moment, and gaped at the flames that were now licking around the wooden crates and barrels stacked in the fo'c'sle. Then, as if at a pre-arranged signal, they all jumped overboard.

As I say, Rosie was astonished at the effectiveness of her plan. It would not be long before she was to discover *why* it had been so effective. For now, however, she span round with a look of triumph, and said: 'Stop it!' to the Doctor, who was just about to start sawing at Nicobobinus's leg. The Doctor turned a bleary, unshaven face towards her, and, for the first time, Rosie noticed that his robes – that had once been lined with fur – were threadbare and stained. And as he peered at her through his thick pebble glasses, Rosie realised that he was as desperate a man as any of them.

'It's gold!' said the Doctor. 'I'm not leaving here without what's due to me!' And he began to saw at Nicobobinus's leg. Nicobobinus screamed, and Rosie leapt on the Doctor.

It was at this moment that Rosie discovered the reason for her scheme being so effective. At the same time, she also discovered the snag. . . . There was an ear-shattering explosion, followed by another and another and another and another and another.

'Oh blimey!' cried Rosie. 'The cargo! It's gunpowder!'

Finding oneself on board an exploding, burning ship would not necessarily be regarded as a stroke of good luck by most people, but, as I say, Rosie wasn't like most people, and she could only see the points in its favour, which were: (1) the Doctor stopped attacking Nicobobinus's leg, (2) he dropped his saw, and (3) he dived under the table.

'I wonder if his medical advice is as bad as his idea of what to do in an emergency?' thought Rosie to herself, as she freed Nicobobinus from the table.

'Let's get out of here!' said Nicobobinus, grabbing his clothes, and racing for the door.

'Help me!' cried the Doctor, as another series of explosions shook the ship, and hurled Rosie and Nicobobinus back against the wall of the poop-deck.

'Phew!' said Nicobobinus, looking at the blazing fo'c'sle, 'Nice work, Rosie!'

At that moment, the whole deck began to tilt, as the great ship began to slide under the waves, and Nicobobinus and Rosie found themselves pitched towards the exploding inferno.

Nicobobinus lost his balance on his golden feet, and tumbled over towards the burning bows, but, as yet another series of kegs began to explode, Rosie hurled herself at full length and just caught his leg with one hand and a trailing rope with the other.

'Help me!' screamed the Doctor, as the door of the Captain's cabin swung open once again, and he came skidding out on his threadbare robe, slithering towards the fo'c'sle.

'Grab this!' cried Nicobobinus, hurling his line towards the wretched man.

But even as they hauled the Doctor back up to the comparative safety of the poop, they heard a splintering sound, and they looked up to see a great black ship bearing down upon them, for - although they didn't know it - this is what had happened. The burning *Santa Margharita* had drifted through the moorings of a neighbouring vessel, and as this ship began to drift free, the *Santa Margharita* had slewed round into her path.

Thus it was that Rosie, Nicobobinus and the despicable Doctor found their ship not only burning, exploding and sinking, but also being sliced neatly in two by another vessel.

'Here we go!' shouted Rosie, and, as the *Santa Margharita* began to break apart, Rosie hurled herself at the

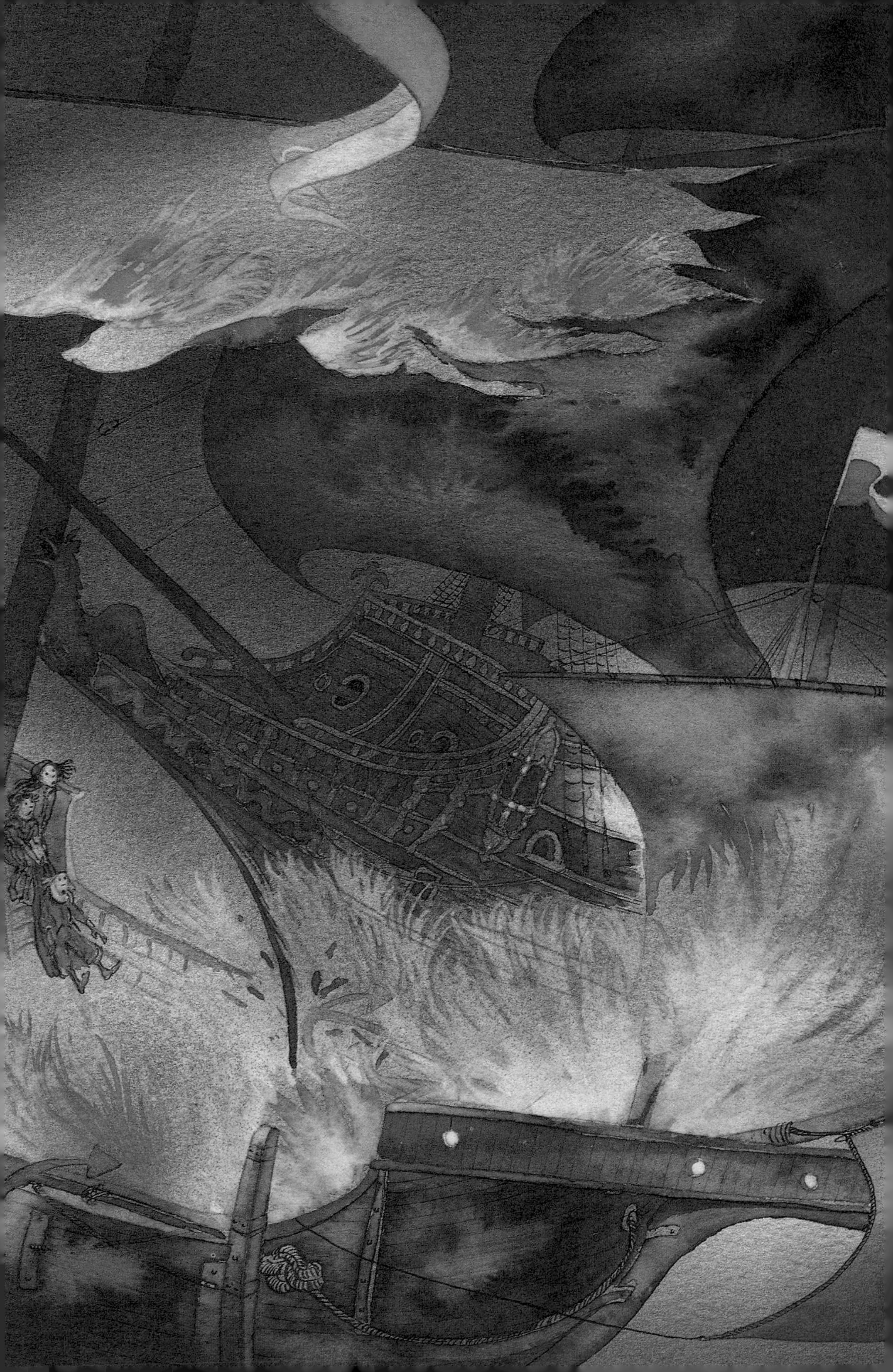

side of the other ship. Nicobobinus and the Doctor looked at each other for a split second, as if to say: 'She must be mad!' and then followed suit.

They were not a moment too soon, for as the black ship sliced her way through the burning hull, the *Santa Margharita* finally sank beneath the waves, leaving only a shower of sparks and a few burning spars.

And so it was that Nicobobinus, Rosie and the unspeakable Dr Sebastian came to find themselves clinging to the outside of a mysterious ship, that was now drifting out of the harbour into the Venetian lagoon.

8

A Rather Long Chapter In Which All Sorts of Things Happen

'Help! Help! Help me! Oh! Merciful Heavens take pity on me! For God's sake have mercy! Somebody help!' The Doctor went on yelling like this for some time. Meanwhile Nicobobinus looked at Rosie and Rosie looked at Nicobobinus.

'Sorry about all this,' said Rosie.

'No! . . . Thanks for rescuing me,' said Nicobobinus. He *had* planned to say something else, but somehow this didn't seem quite the moment.

'I expect the crew will hear him any moment,' said Rosie, nodding at the Doctor, who was still yelling his head off.

'I hope they do,' said Nicobobinus. 'I don't know how much longer I can hold on for.'

The truth was Nicobobinus was having the very devil of a job trying to stop his golden feet slipping off the sodden rubbing strake, on which they were perched, as they clung to the gunwales. He was finding it especially difficult now, for as the ship was beginning to lurch from side to side as the strong current swept her out of the lagoon. And he knew and Rosie knew that, if he fell off, his golden feet would drag him under the waves like two stone weights.

'I can't hold on!' cried Nicobobinus.

'Where's the crew?' shouted Rosie. 'Are they all asleep?'

'Mary, Mother of Jesus, protect and forgive me in this hour of need!' screamed the Doctor.

'Oh shut up!' said Rosie, and then, as she noticed Nicobobinus's feet slip from under him as the ship rolled again, she yelled at the top of her voice: 'Help! Somebody help!'

'I just can't get a grip!' cried Nicobobinus.

It was at that moment that Rosie noticed that the Doctor was actually clinging to some rigging.

'That creep!' she cried. 'Can't you get over to that rigging he's keeping to himself, Nico?'

'I'll try!' said Nicobobinus, and he began edging his way towards the Doctor.

Just then the ship rolled again.

'I'm dead!' whimpered the Doctor, clinging to the sheets with his eyes shut tight. 'This is it! The wretched end of a wretched life!'

'You idiot!' yelled Nicobobinus, as he just managed to get his one hand on the rope that the Doctor had hold of.

'What is it?' shouted Rosie, above the crashing of the waves, which seemed to be getting rougher every minute.

'Get off my ropes!' snarled the Doctor, aiming a kick at Nicobobinus.

'Look! You idiot!' cried Nicobobinus. 'There's a port-hole straight in front of you, only you're in such a panic you can't see it!'

If Dr Sebastian had been good at thinking up sharp

retorts, I'm sure he would have said something so cutting – so wounding – that Nicobobinus would never have dared to call him an idiot again or to point out his failings for all and sundry to hear. As it was, however, the only thing the Doctor could think of was: 'Gmpf!' and as he realised this wasn't particularly cutting or wounding he kept it to himself. And instead of deigning to reply, he dived head-first through the porthole. Nicobobinus followed suit, and Rosie wasn't far behind.

Once on the deck of the ship, they all three collapsed exhausted. Rosie must have fallen fast asleep, for when she woke up it was day. The sun was shining over the vast blue sea, a gentle breeze was blowing, and it was all exactly as she had planned it might be, when she had first suggested they look for the Land of Dragons . . . except that she was tied up. She craned her neck round, and there was Nicobobinus in the same situation. The Doctor was nowhere to be seen.

'He's looking for a saw,' said Nicobobinus cheerfully.

'He's out of his head,' replied Rosie.

At that moment, the Doctor evidently found what he was looking for, because there was a whoop of what might have passed for joy in the Doctor's thin, grey heart. A few minutes later, he reappeared on deck, beaming like the Doge giving out bread at the Orphanage, and brandishing a long saw.

'It's no use you screaming!' he grinned. 'I've been from end to end of this boat, and there's not a soul on it!'

'That's shocking!' said Nicobobinus. 'It's against the regulations to leave a ship unattended in the harbour.'

'Shut up!' said the Doctor. 'That's irrelevant.'

'No it isn't,' replied Nicobobinus. 'It's important to have at least three people on board in case of an emergency.'

'I don't care,' said the Doctor. 'I'm going to get my gold ... all of it!' And he came up to Nicobobinus, and raised the saw over his leg.

'But this is an emergency!' cried Nicobobinus. 'We're adrift at sea without a crew – you'll need all three of us to have any chance of getting safe to land!'

The Doctor paused for a moment. But just then the sun glinted on Nicobobinus's golden feet, and it glistened in the Doctor's eyes, and he could think of nothing else.

'Gold is gold!' he said. 'I'll have my due!' And he placed the saw on Nicobobinus's leg.

'You idiot!' cried Rosie.

'Don't call me that!' screamed the Doctor, turning on her. 'I'm not an idiot! I could have passed my examinations if I'd studied harder!'

'You mean you're not even a fully qualified surgeon?' exclaimed Nicobobinus indignantly.

'It doesn't matter,' said the Doctor. 'This gold will make me as rich as any of them!'

'I refuse to allow you to touch my leg until you're properly .qualified!' said Nicobobinus, without many expectations.

'Shut up!' cried the Doctor. 'It always puts me off when the patient talks.'

'Stop!' cried Rosie, as the Doctor began to saw. 'You're cutting off your nose to spite your face!'

For the first time in his life of failure, a witty reply popped into the Doctor's head. Well, it wasn't exactly what you or I might have called a witty reply, but he was tremendously pleased with it.

'Oh no,' he said, 'I'm cutting off *his feet* to fill *my* pocket!'

'You misunderstand,' said Rosie.

'Shut up!' snapped the Doctor, who was rather piqued that neither Rosie nor Nicobobinus were doubled-up with laughter in appreciation of his witty reply. 'It's you that didn't understand . . . I'm cutting off *his* feet to . . .'

'Yes, yes, I got it the first time,' said Rosie.

'Well why didn't you laugh?'

'Ha ha,' said Nicobobinus.

The Doctor gave a slight bow, and raised his saw again.

'But if you cut off his feet and his hand and the back of his neck . . .'

'Ooh! I hadn't noticed that!' said the Doctor.

'. . . he'll bleed to death!' said Rosie.

'Well that's his look out,' replied the Doctor.

'But don't you want even *more* gold?' asked Rosie.

Nothing - absolutely nothing - Rosie could have said was as likely to have grabbed the Doctor's full attention.

'What's that?' he said.

'Well if he dies, how can he grow any more gold?' asked Rosie.

The Doctor hesitated, and stared at Nicobobinus. 'You mean . . .' he said, 'he *grew* all this gold?'

'How else d'you think he got like that?' said Rosie, thinking very quickly. 'It's a rare medical disease.'

'Well *I've* never heard of it,' replied the Doctor.

'*You* didn't pass your exams!' said Nicobobinus.

'But I *know* there's no such disease!' said the Doctor.

'But you've never seen anyone whose feet have turned to gold before!' replied Rosie.

'That's true,' said the Doctor.

'It's like I said,' Rosie went on, improvising freely, 'a *very, very* rare disease - it's so rare you wouldn't have been expected to know about it. It's called . . . Deathgold . . . and the longer you leave it the worse it gets.'

'You mean . . .' said the Doctor, his eyes slowly becoming as big as saucers. 'You mean . . . *other* bits of him will turn to gold??'

'His whole body will turn to gold, unless we can find a cure . . .'

'Oh no no no! I'm sure there's no cure . . . it's not even worth looking,' said the Doctor.

'I thought you didn't know the disease?' said Nicobobinus.

'Er . . . I'm beginning to remember a bit about it,' said the Doctor.

'Like how bad exercise is for it?' said Rosie.

'Is it?' said the Doctor.

'Oh yes – you remember! The more you move around, the faster you turn into gold,' said Rosie. And before they could say 'Mice!' the Doctor was untying Nicobobinus.

'There . . . there we are . . . have a nice run around!' he said, and he made Nicobobinus run around the deck for the rest of the day. Every time Nicobobinus passed by where Rosie was still lying tied up, he murmured out of the corner of his mouth: 'Thanks a lot, Rosie!' And she couldn't quite work out what he meant. . . .

The black ship continued to drift all day. The Doctor found the wine store, and sat on deck drinking and watching Nicobobinus run around under the hot sun. Every so often he would stop him, and examine him to see if any more parts had begun to turn to gold.

Meanwhile, the ship wallowed and drifted and rolled and tossed as a stiff wind got up. And the dreadful Doctor drank more and more wine, and began cursing Nicobobinus and throwing the bottles at Rosie, until he slumped into a drunken stupor.

As soon as he was snoring soundly, Nicobobinus untied Rosie.

'I think we should return the favour, don't you?' he said, and the two of them lashed the drunken Doctor to the mast.

'Right!' said Nicobobinus. 'Which way's the Land of Dragons! I'm sick of having golden feet!'

'China's where they come from, isn't it?' said Rosie, who had worked all this out ages ago.

'Right!' said Nicobobinus. 'East it is!' And he charged off below decks to find the tiller.

It was at that very moment, however, that Rosie saw something which was to change their plans considerably.

'Nico!' she yelled. But Nicobobinus was deep down in the stern, staring at the tiller.

'It moved without me touching it!' he exclaimed, as Rosic appeared.

'There's another ship sailing towards us!' she cried.

'The tiller turned and altered course without me doing anything!' said Nicobobinus. 'And look!' He pointed at a wooden bowl of water that stood on a table near the tiller.

'What's that?' asked Rosie.

'Well,' said Nicobobinus. 'It's the very latest scientific invention. You see that twig floating in the water?'

'Yes,' said Rosie who hadn't but did now.

'Well,' said Nicobobinus, 'It's got a little bit of metal in the end that always points North . . .'

'Like a compass,' said Rosie.

'It *is* a compass,' said Nicobobinus (who was a little bit cheesed off that Rosie already knew all about it).

'I've got a cousin who makes them,' said Rosie, looking at it critically. 'This one's a bit crude.'

'But d'you see, if that's North, we're heading East!' exclaimed Nicobobinus to change the subject. 'It's almost as if the boat knew which way we wanted to go!'

'On the other hand, maybe it's just getting away from the other ship,' said Rosie.

'What other ship?' asked Nicobobinus.

'I told you – the one that's coming towards us, and it's quite close.'

At that moment there was a crash, and the whole boat shuddered.

'Uh oh!' said Rosie 'I think it's arrived!'

'Crumbs!' said Nicobobinus, as a series of mighty clangs shook the deck above them, and bloodthirsty cries filled the air. 'We're being boarded!'

'You'd better hide!' cried Rosie, as footsteps thundered over their heads and began cascading down gangways and ladders.

'Pirates!' cried Nicobobinus, as the door splintered apart, and in burst three monks brandishing cutlasses.

'Kids!' said the first monk.

'Yeah!' said the second. 'Kids!'

And they all three turned and disappeared into the bowels of the ship.

Rosie looked at Nicobobinus in total incomprehension, and said: '*Monks*?'

'They *can't* be!' said Nicobobinus, and they both hurried up onto the deck.

9

Pirates!

Men were running here, there and everywhere, smashing open hatchways, ripping through shrouds, and frantically breaking open bales and boxes. More of them were still leaping across from their own ship, which had been secured alongside with grappling irons, and yet more of them were swarming over the rails of the black ship, knives in their mouths and cutlasses ready in their hands.

The thing that most amazed Nicobobinus and Rosie, however, was the fact that each and every one of these wild-looking characters wore the cowl and habit of a monk, and each had his hair cut in a tonsure. In the centre of the deck stood the Abbot. He was dressed in red robes, and was interrogating the whining Dr Sebastian.

'Of course it's my ship!' the Doctor was screaming. 'I was overpowered and my crew murdered before my very eyes! I tell you!'

'Calm yourself, my dear fellow,' the Abbot was saying. 'We are crusaders – not pirates.'

'Then go and attack the heathens!' whined the Doctor.

'But we are! Should we find that either ship or cargo

belongs to Heathen, Turk or Jew, we shall confiscate it'.

'But it's mine!' screamed the Doctor.

'And perhaps *you're* a heathen!' beamed the Abbot. 'But we shall soon find out with a little questioning. ...'

'Torture!' screamed the Doctor. 'I can't bear torture!'

At this point, Nicobobinus and Rosie felt themselves grabbed from behind, and propelled towards the Abbot.

'Ah! I see you've brought your children with you,' said the Abbot. 'They will soon tell me whether you're Christian or not.'

'Them? They're the ones that started it!' screamed the Doctor. 'They're bloodthirsty heathens – the pair of them!'

'Indeed?' said the Abbot.

'Throw 'em overboard, your Holiness?' asked the monk who was holding Rosie.

'Certainly *not*!' replied the Abbot. 'No monk of our order must ever be stained with the innocent blood of a

Christian child. We must carry out a proper investigation into this gentleman's charges, and then deal with the children accordingly. You must never just "throw people overboard", Brother Bartholomew!'

'Oh .... no? ... sorry, your Holiness,' said the monk.

'Is that *gold*?' asked the Abbot, peering at Nicobobinus's hand.

'It's mine!' screamed the Doctor.

'It's on *his* arm,' pointed out the Abbot.

'But it's been promised to me!'

'Well, child?' said the Abbot, smiling in his kindly way at Nicobobinus. '*Have* you promised your hand to this gentleman?'

'No sir,' replied Nicobobinus, and immediately felt a heavy clout on the back of his head.

'No, *Your Holiness*!' said the monk who was holding him.

'Ow!' said Nicobobinus, and got another clout.

'Ow! *Your Holiness*!' said the monk.

'Good,' said the Abbot. 'Gold is a sacred trust sent to us from God. It should neither be acquired nor disposed of lightly.'

'I just want to change my hand and feet back to normal,' said Nicobobinus, and got another clout on the back of his head. 'Your Holiness,' he added.

Clearly the Abbot hadn't noticed Nicobobinus's feet, for he now gave a low whistle.

'My word!' he murmured. 'You certainly *would* be an asset to the Abbey ...'

'He's mine!' screamed the desperate Doctor, struggling to get free.

The Abbot turned and smiled at the monks holding Dr Sebastian. 'This gentleman does indeed deserve God's mercy, does he not?' he said. 'And who are we to deny him the joy of eternal bliss?'

'Do you mean "throw him overboard", Your Holiness?' asked one of the monks.

The Abbot coughed, and then said: 'Brother Anselm! You must pray for God's guidance in this as in all matters and trust that He will instruct your hand to act in accordance with His will.'

Brother Anselm waited for a moment, and then threw Dr Sebastian overboard.

'I say!' said Rosie.

'Gosh!' said Nicobobinus.

'Benedictus, benedicat. Per Jesum Christum, dominum nostrum, Amen,' said the Abbot, and the entire crew crossed themselves.

'*Poor* fellow,' said the Abbot, shaking his head. 'Let us trust that he will find salvation in the Life Hereafter.'

'He wasn't very nice – but I don't think you should have done *that* to him!' said Rosie.

But the Abbot didn't hear her, or if he did he didn't take any notice, for he had climbed the steps to the quarter-deck, and was now addressing the crew.

'My sons,' he said, 'I have grave news for you all. It seems that God, in His wisdom, has called to His side the owner of this vessel, and so He has entrusted the entire ship and its cargo into our safe-keeping. Let us pray that we shall prove ourselves worthy of His trust.'

All the monks cheered and waved their cutlasses in the air. 'Amen,' said the Abbot, and the two ships turned towards the East.

10

How Nicobobinus Received an Offer He Couldn't Refuse

Rosie and Nicobobinus were locked in a cupboard where they sat in the pitch dark, listening to the creak of the ship and the squeak of the rats. Nevertheless, Rosie remained surprisingly cheerful.

'You know,' she said to Nicobobinus, as one of the ship's timbers slipped of its own accord, allowing the sun to flood in, 'I can't help feeling this ship's very odd.'

Nicobobinus didn't reply, because the sunlight had revealed a loose plank, and he was busy prising it up. Underneath they found a stash of wine and some amazingly fresh cakes.

'Well it's being very nice to us,' said Nicobobinus in between mouthfuls.

Some days later, Rosie and Nicobobinus looked out of their peep hole and saw land ahead. The two ships were brought into harbour, and, for the first time since their capture, the door of their cupboard was opened up and one of the monks looked in. He seemed quite surprised to see the two children.

'You still alive?' was the only thing he said as he dragged them before the Abbot. The Abbot was in the middle of a huge meal. There were dishes of spiced liver, sweetbreads in milk, lamb's brains, oxes hearts, stewed tripes, grilled kidneys and several blood puddings. The Abbot was the only one eating, although he was surrounded by servants who wiped his mouth, poured his wine and cut up the large pieces of offal.

When he saw the two children the Abbot frowned for a moment.

'They're still alive!' said the monk.

The Abbot looked rather irritated and replied: 'I can see that, thank you, Brother Anselm.' Then he shovelled a large piece of tongue into his mouth and apparently swallowed it whole, while he gazed at the two children, and in particular at Nicobobinus's golden appendages. Then quite suddenly he smiled a warm, golden smile – so soft and loving that you couldn't help smiling back, and he said: 'My children, I trust you have had a pleasant voyage?'

'We were locked in a cupboard,' said Rosie.

The Abbot looked horrified. 'No!' he said. 'Brother Anselm! Can this be true?'

'Well . . . er . . . yes . . .' said Brother Anselm.

'But that's disgraceful! If I had only known, my child, it *is* quite solid is it?' He was now tapping Nicobobinus's golden hand with his spoon.

'Yes . . .' said Nicobobinus, '. . . er . . . Your Holiness!'

The Abbot stared at Nicobobinus for some moments as if he were weighing him out, golden ounce by golden ounce. Then he suddenly stood up and looked out of the window. When he turned back he was smiling again.

'My child! I have wonderful news for you!'

Nicobobinus felt a sinking feeling in the pit of his stomach, but Rosie squeezed his hand, and he knew what she was saying to him in her mind.

'God has called you!' beamed the Abbot.

'They're going to throw me overboard!' thought Nicobobinus.

'Not if I can help it!' thought Rosie.

'He has commanded us to admit you into the Most Holy Order of St Francis,' said the Abbot.

'But I don't want to be a monk!' exclaimed Nicobobinus, and then just before he was hit on the back of the head, he added: 'Your Holiness!' But it was too late. He was hit on the back of the head anyway.

11

Nicobobinus's First and Only Day as a Monk

And so it was that Nicobobinus woke up one bright spring morning to find himself a novitiate monk in the Monastery of St Francis in the town of Segna in the land of the Uskoks.

His head was sore where his hair had been shaved off, and he was extremely hungry. His cell was magnificently furnished for an early cave dweller: the bare walls went down to the bare floor, and there was nothing else in it apart from the thin blanket in which Nicobobinus found himself.

A bell was tolling over the great courtyard and he could hear footsteps outside. Suddenly a key turned in the lock and his door was thrown open.

'Breakfast,' said a monk who might have been Brother Anselm, and led Nicobobinus across the courtyard and up the Grand Staircase to the Refectory, where all the other monks were standing saying grace.

'Benedictus benedicat. Per Jesum Christum, dominum nostrum, Amen, ' said the Abbot, and they all sat down to eat.

Nicobobinus, however, was led before the Abbot. He stood there for some time, while the Abbot chewed on half a dozen chickens' necks. Finally, however, the great man looked up and smiled his warm smile.

'Ah, my child! We do hope you are going to be happy here,' he said.

'I'll be very much happier when I've had some breakfast, Your Holiness,' said Nicobobinus.

All the monks stopped eating and looked up at him. The Abbot coughed: 'Ah! My dear child, I'm afraid it is against the rules of the Order for a novitiate monk of the Order of St Francis to eat breakfast.'

'When is lunch then, Your Holiness?' asked Nicobobinus.

'It is a hard calling. I'm afraid lunch and supper are also forbidden to novitiate monks.'

'When do they eat then . . . Your Holiness?' asked Nicobobinus.

'They offer their appetites as a sacrifice to God,' replied the Abbot.

'I'm sorry?' said Nicobobinus.

'They eschew food entirely until they are admitted fully into the Order.'

'And how long does that take?' asked Nicobobinus.

The Abbot smiled warmly: 'Only a couple of years.'

'But I'll have starved to death by then!' said Nicobobinus.

'Let us hope *not*,' said the Abbot, looking *very* concerned, and all the other monks crossed themselves and murmured: 'Amen'.

Nicobobinus looked around at them and then said: 'May I ask, Your Holiness, how all these monks survived their time as novitiates?'

The Abbot coughed and the other monks suddenly became very interested in their food again.

'It's a new rule,' beamed the Abbot. 'You have the honour of being the first to observe it!'

'And when I've starved to death, you'll have the honour of sticking my hand and my feet in your coffers!' exclaimed Nicobobinus.

'Well . . . it is true,' sighed the Abbot, 'that your body and possessions belong to the Abbey, and will naturally be put to the service of God . . .'

'You're a lot of hypocrites!' cried Nicobobinus, and several monks choked over their plates.

'You're just pirates and robbers! And I'm not staying here a moment longer!'

And with that he dived under the Abbot's table, grabbed the great man's legs and up-ended the lot.

The chicken neck, on which the Abbot had been sucking, shot straight down his throat and became firmly wedged in his windpipe. The Abbot spluttered and gasped and his eyes bulged as he rose to his feet clutching his gorge.

And this is where the Abbot's past caught up with him, I'm afraid. For the truth is that despite his mild manner and infectious laugh, the monks all held him in mortal dread. They feared the slightest raising of his eyebrow, they trembled at his smile, and now here he was flailing his arms and getting redder and redder - and becoming in truth apoplectic, and the terror at what must be going through his mind totally paralysed every monk there. They simply stood and gawped. And Nicobobinus didn't waste a moment. He was on his feet and dropping out of the window before the Abbot's face could turn blue.

You may have noticed that 'dropping' is one of the most difficult things to stop when you're half-way through, and yet that's exactly what Nicobobinus wanted to do, the moment he dropped from the window of the Abbot's Refectory. The reason he wanted to was that he suddenly remembered the Refectory was on the second floor, and it was a long ... long way to the ground. In fact it was the sort of distance one might drop a dinosaur egg to see if you could crack it. And dinosaur eggs - as you probably know - are about the same size and thickness as the human skull. So in principle Nicobobinus was probably as wise to think about stopping dropping as he had been unwise to start dropping in the first place.

At this point I have to tell you that the Abbot's kitchen garden was one of the things that gave the Abbot the greatest pleasure in life - second only to robbing merchant ships on the high seas, under the pretence that they belonged to heathens. Now the man who tended the Abbot's kitchen garden was named Melchior, and it was Melchior's little joke that, like one of the three wise men bringing the gifts to Christ in the manger, so he was always bringing gifts to the Abbot's table.

At this precise instant, however, Melchior was driving a cartload of dung from the Abbot's stable to the Abbot's kitchen garden. And it was by one of those flukes of fate that he happened to be passing under the very window from which Nicobobinus was dropping, at the very moment that Nicobobinus decided he would like to stop dropping. And thus it was that Nicobobinus managed to stop dropping exactly when he wanted to, and, instead, landed in a cartload of high-class excrement.

Melchior knew nothing of all this, however, because Nicobobinus did not yell out, and because in any case,

Melchior was a trifle deaf, and also because Melchior made it his business *never* to look up to heaven, as long as he was in the service of the Abbot's table.

By the time the monks looked down out of the Refectory window, Melchior's cart had turned the corner and Nicobobinus, whom they expected to see spread out – sunny-side up – on the paved courtyard below, had quite simply disappeared. The name Basilcat, for some reason, came to the lips of one young novice, but he could not think why, and he never thought of it again. It was just one of those things.

Now some of you may have been wondering what had happened to Rosie all this time. Well, at the very moment that Nicobobinus stopped dropping out of the window, Rosie was just nearing the end of what was, perhaps, the most incredible adventure in this whole story. This is what had happened.

12

Rosie and the Black Ship

When the two ships had tied up in the harbour, Nicobobinus had been carted off by the monks, kicking and struggling. Rosie too bit and scratched them as they carried him off, but no matter what she did no-one took the slightest notice of her. 'I suppose it's because I'm only a girl,' she said to herself, because that's what everyone told her, although personally Rosie couldn't see that it ought to make the slightest difference. Eventually, however, they locked her back in the cupboard.

She sat there, miserable and angry.

'They only want Nicobobinus's gold,' she moaned. 'They'll cut his feet off . . .' But she could hardly think any more because of the banging and clattering going on all over the boat. It sounded just as if the monks were stripping the ship bare, which was, as a matter of fact, exactly what they were doing.

It was night before all was quiet again. Rosie sat in the pitch dark. She was tired and thirsty and hungry, but most of all she was desperately anxious about Nicobobinus. 'How can I rescue him if I can't even get out of this stupid cupboard?' she muttered, as she rattled the door. And then the first odd thing happened. The door simply opened – just like that – as if it had never been locked in the first place.

At first Rosie wasn't quite sure what had happened, because, as I said, it was pitch dark, and she couldn't actually see that the door had swung open – she could only feel it. Then the second odd thing happened – and, as far as Rosie was concerned, this was perhaps the creepiest of all. As she felt around in the blackness, a candle in one of the lanterns slowly sputtered into life. Rosie stopped and stared – fascinated. Then she took the lantern and began to explore the ship. Everything had been picked clean – as if a plague of locusts had swept through the boat. There was not a crate nor a bale of cargo and not a stick of furniture. Everything removable had gone, and even things that weren't really removable had been torn out.

Eventually Rosie made her way up onto the main deck. 'Let's get off this spooky boat, and start looking for Nicobobinus!' she muttered. But the stiff breeze cut through her dress, and she shivered, as she looked out into the pitch blackness of the night. And her heart sank as she realised she didn't have the first idea of how to get off the ship – she didn't even know on which side lay the land and on which side the deep ocean.

'Perhaps I'd better wait until it's light,' she muttered, and retreated below decks. There she found another candle burning in the galley, and then she discovered the third odd thing. On the table in the galley was a steaming hot plate of food complete with a knife and spoon – all laid out ready.

'How did those vultures come to miss *that*?' she wondered, 'and how come it's so hot?'

Well she didn't stop to think any more about it, because it was spaghetti with cockles in tomato sauce. And when she'd polished it off she couldn't help looking round to see if the cook was still around - and there, to her amazement, was a mug of warm milk, standing on the side table.

'How did you know! That's just what I wanted!' exclaimed Rosie, and then she laughed as she realised she was talking to the ship.

'I must be going mad' she thought to herself. 'But it's just as if the boat were looking after me . . .'

At that moment, however, she heard a door bang on the quarter-deck above, so she quickly hid under the chopping board. She lay there still as a mouse, for some minutes, but she heard nothing else. The ship was quite quiet. At last she ventured out of the galley and climbed the steps to the quarter-deck. There she caught her breath, for she could see a light shining in the Captain's cabin. She tiptoed across the quarter-deck, and cautiously peered in at the Captain's window. Now if I had been Rosie, I don't suppose I would have done that. I would have left well alone. But that wasn't Rosie's way of doing things. And there again if I had been Rosie, I wouldn't have discovered what Rosie did: the Captain's cabin was untouched. All the furnishings were there intact. The covers of the bunk were turned down ready for her, and a nightlight glowed softly on the table.

'Thank you, Black Ship,' said Rosie, as she laid her head on the pillow. And the candles blew themselves out, and Rosie felt the great ship move. And she heard cables running across the deck, and chains pulling up over the sides, but it all felt so much like a dream that she didn't wake up, and the anchor dropped softly to the deck and she swayed as the breeze caught the sails and the Black Ship turned in the darkness. . . .

When Rosie woke up she screamed with fright, for there . . . but hold on a minute! I really ought to tell you what happened to Nicobobinus first, and you'll see why later.

13

How Brother Michael Helped Nicobobinus Escape

Now you may remember that Nicobobinus had landed upside-down in a dung-cart being driven by Melchior, the Abbot's gardener. Well it so happened that Melchior had done a most unpleasant thing to the pretty girl who helped in the kitchen. He had given her a bad cucumber. The reason he had done this is far from clear, and is not really relevant. The point is, that Angela, the kitchen girl, was betrothed to Nicholas, the wainwright, and this is why one of the wheels of the dung-cart suddenly came loose and rolled off down the hill. For, as I'm sure you know, a wainwright not only makes wagons and carts, but he also repairs them. So when Melchior took his dung-cart to Nicholas the wainwright for its annual service, Nicholas extracted a little revenge for the bad cucumber by extracting one of the little pins holding the wheels of the cart. And he told Angela what he had done later that night. So, today, when Angela saw the wheel rolling past the open door of the Abbot's kitchen, she smiled and lifted her eyes to heaven, and devoutly thanked God for giving her such a good man as Nicholas.

As a matter of fact, the wheel continued to roll on, out of the abbey gates and down the hill into the village, and it rolled right into the wainwright's shop, and Nicholas too smiled when he saw it, and he too raised his eyes to heaven and thanked God for making him such a clever fellow. . . .

It was, you see, a town full of devout people, who loathed bad cucumbers.

The cost of repairing his runaway wheel was, however, the last thought on Melchior's mind at that precise moment. His thoughts were running on the lines of: 'Oh no! Damn! Blast it!' and so forth and so on, as the wagon slumped over to one side and then veered across into the wall of the kitchen garden and deposited its entire contents right across the Abbot's Lawn!

'Boiling oil dripped on my bare back!' thought Melchior to himself. 'Fingernails pulled out on alternate fingers every other day, and then pushed down my throat with red hot tongs on Sunday! That's what the Abbot'll do to me! *And* he's having a lawn party here this afternoon! Goodbye fingernails! Goodbye skin on my back!'

He then opened his eyes and looked at the dung all over the beautiful grass sward – and he nearly had a heart attack there and then, for some of it suddenly got up, ran across the lawn and jumped over the kitchen garden wall.

As for Nicobobinus himself, he wouldn't have been the least surprised that someone mistook him for a piece of living manure – that's exactly what he felt like, as he raced across the Abbot's kitchen garden, and headed for the back gates of the abbey. The only trouble was – the abbey had no back gates, as Nicobobinus discovered, the moment he skidded round the corner of the wash house and saw the high stone wall blocking his way.

'Damn!' he said, and doubled back, only to find that

a number of the younger monks had by now appeared from the Refectory.

'There he is!' cried the youngest, pointing to the leaping dung heap that was now racing towards the Chapter House.

Nicobobinus didn't stop to count how many of them exclaimed: 'Urggh!' or 'It can't be!' He just ran.

He ran into the Chapter House, and left a trail of stinking footsteps right across the marble floor. And he ran through the door that led into the Parlour, where the Cellarer and several of the largest brethren were arguing with the town butcher about the price of the latest load of offal which he had just delivered. The Cellarer, whose name was Hugh, stopped in mid-tirade (about the mortal sin of avarice) as Nicobobinus ran past, arms pumping, ordure flying this way and that, and then disappeared into the Cloisters.

Here Nicobobinus found his way had been blocked, by another group of monks who had been despatched by the Abbot. These monks had had time to grab various weapons, such as carving-knives, meat-cleavers and a soup ladle. Nicobobinus didn't think it was worth stopping to ask what the monk with the soup ladle intended doing with it, he just looked for another door out of the Cloister. He looked behind him, he looked in front of him, he looked to his left, he looked to his right and at last he knew the answer: there wasn't one.

'Uh-oh!' muttered Nicobobinus as the younger monks suddenly burst into the Cloister behind him and the monks with the knives began to advance towards him. 'This is going to be one of those dazzling escapes for which I am not yet famous!' And with that he hurled himself at one of the pillars of the colonnade supporting the Cloister roof, and began to swarm up it. Here, he discovered that being disguised as an animated compost heap has one other draw-back in addition to the smell: it makes shinning up a per-fectly smooth stone column very, very difficult. This is especially so if you happen to have one golden hand and two golden feet. Thus, as his pursuers closed in on him from all sides, Nicobobinus found himself slipping down the pillar, and the faster he tried to climb the further he slipped down.

'Give me a couple more days of this,' thought Nico-bobinus, 'and I could probably climb up as far as the bottom!'

However, I now have to tell you a frightful thing about one of the monks. His name was Michael, and he had developed a most shameful vice. Everyone in the monastery was aware that this particular vice had gripped one of their number, but no-one yet had a clue as to who it could be. However, had they observed in the group of older monks the one who carried the soup ladle, they might have realised at this very moment that it was he, Brother Michael, for he blanched as Nicobobinus too discovered his secret vice.

And now I have to tell you Brother Michael's shameful secret. This is it. He stole out of the dormitory at dead of night, armed with a knife and . . . I can hardly bear to say it . . . and . . . he would *carve his initials on the monastery walls*!

Now you might object that if he carved his initials, it would be a simple matter for the other monks to find out who he was. There is, however, a perfectly rational explanation as to why his initials did *not* reveal his identity, but if you want to bother with such a tedious and, to my mind, totally unnecessary explanation you will have to look up the footnote at the bottom of this page, since having to stop and explain it all now would simply get in the way of the story. The footnote, by the way, is marked by this little asterisk here.* Now, while the pedants are reading the footnote, the rest of us can get on with the tale.

Brother Michael had, I'm afraid, executed one of his grandest carvings on the very pillar of the cloister colon-

---

* For those who insist on pursuing this ridiculous quibble as to why Brother Michael's initials didn't give him away, the reason is simply this: his first initial was B for Brother, and as everyone, apart from the Abbot, was called Brother that meant nothing. His second initial, of course, was M, but that gave away nothing either since the abbey had over 60 other monks whose names began with M. It was one of those strange freaks of nature, with which life is full, and there is no explanation as to why there were so many of them, but there it is. There were: Macanisius, Macartan, Machabees, Machalus, Machor, Machutus, Madron, Maedoc, Maelruain (an Irish monk), Malrubius, Magnus (who came from the Isle of Orkney),

nade, up which Nicobobinus was now trying to shin. He had cut the initial M particularly deeply, and, because it was a nice night, and the wine at dinner had been particularly strong, he had finished it off by underlining it. And it was into this deep fissure, underlining the M, that Nicobobinus's golden foot now accidentally slipped. It fitted perfectly. And suddenly he had a foothold.

What is more, for this particular work, Brother Michael had adopted a slightly old fashioned form of lettering known as the uncial, and consequently his M was carved in this fashion: m thus affording another foothold for Nicobobinus's golden foot. Furthermore, since the column was rather slender and delicate, Brother Michael had carved his B *above* the M rather than alongside it, thereby providing Nicobobinus with three more footholds, into which he inserted his golden feet . . . 1 . . . 2 . . . 3 . . . and Up!

And so it was thanks to Brother Michael's disgraceful weakness for lettering that Nicobobinus suddenly found himself – against all the odds – on the roof of the Cloister of the abbey at Segna in the land of the Uskoks.

Over the tiles he ran, with knives and meat cleavers whistling through the air and smashing the tiles behind him. But he dodged and weaved this way and that, until

---

Majella, Malachy (another Irishman), Malo, Manaccus, Marcellus (from Rome), Marcoul (a Norman), Mark, Martinian, Matthew, Matthias, Maurice (who also came from Rome), Maurus, Maeves, Mawgan (a Welshman), Mawnan (a Cornishman), Mayne (a Devonshireman), Medard (a Frenchman), Mel, Melaine, Mellitus, Mellow, Mennas (an Egyptian), Meriaseh, Methodius, Menbred, Mewan, fifteen other Michaels, Mirin, Mochta, Mochumna, Modan (from Falkirk), Modestus, Modomnoc, Molaise, Moling, Milna, Montfort, Munchin, Murtagh, Mybard and Mylor (although, strictly speaking, Mylor had been expelled from the Order for being kind to animals, so he perhaps shouldn't be counted).

one of the missiles suddenly caught him fair and square right between the shoulder-blades!

'Lucky the only good shot was the one with the soup ladle!' thought Nicobobinus, as he carried on running over the tiles and then jumped across onto the roof of the Lay brothers' Lodging House, climbed to the ridge and then slid down the other side, faster than he meant, and landed in a crumpled heap on the ground below.

'Phew!' said Nicobobinus. 'That was a narrow ...' And he never said 'escape' or even 'squeak', because as he began to pick himself up, he found his nose pressed against one of the most expensive shoes he'd ever had it pressed against, and when he looked up to apologise for smudging ordure onto such a fine piece of leather, he found himself gazing into the distinctly chilly eyes of . . . the Abbot.

'Perhaps you are not suited to monastic life, after all,' said the Abbot. Then he turned to the Cellarer and the other monks who were just about to throw the butcher down the well, and said: 'Bring the boy to the cage.'

14

How Nicobobinus Had the Most Extraordinary Good Luck

Now the abbey at Segna enjoys the most splendid location. Perched over the steep cliffs that guard the Velebitski Kanal, it commands breathtaking views across to the islands of Krk, Prvic, Grgur and Goli. And on a clear day you can even see Rab and Cres. For a city boy like Nicobobinus, who had lived all his life in the narrow streets of Venice, the splendour of such a panorama was enough to make him feel dizzy. This dizziness may of course have been exaggerated by the fact that he was also at that moment locked in an iron cage suspended from the cliff over the sheer drop into the water below.

The Abbot blessed Nicobobinus's soul and commended him to God, and the other monks mumbled something in Latin that again sounded suspiciously like their grace at dinner. Then they all trooped off, leaving poor Nicobobinus hanging there, drinking in the view.

'Why don't they just push me over the edge?' he shouted at the young novice who was still securing the rope at the top.

'His Holiness the Abbot won't allow any of the

Brothers to be stained with the guilt of causing a child's death!' the novice shouted back cheerfully.

'Who's going to do it then?' yelled Nicobobinus, for he couldn't believe they'd suspended him in this cage over the sea without at least some intention of dropping him in.

'These little fellows,' grinned the novice, holding up a cage of rats.

'How do you mean?' shouted Nicobobinus.

'You'll see!' smiled the novice, and he placed the rats' cage so that the rope that held Nicobobinus's cage ran through it.

'Do you get it?' asked the novice. 'It's the Abbot's own invention. When the rats get hungry, they'll gnaw the rope and eventually ...' He mimed Nicobobinus's rapid descent into the sea. 'The currents round here will pull the cage down and wash you up on the beach over there in about a week's time.'

'Charming!' said Nicobobinus.

'None of the brothers is directly guilty of bumping you off, and when the Abbot holds an investigation, he finds that the rats are to blame. So he tries the rats, finds them guilty and executes them ... after torture of course.'

'The rotten egg!' said Nicobobinus – not without some justification.

'So long!' grinned the novice. 'Oh ... and ... sorry!'

And he disappeared back towards the abbey.

Nicobobinus took stock of his situation. He couldn't see any way out of it. The cage was made of thick iron bars, and the door was locked with three padlocks. Clearly it would sink like a stone when it hit the water, and there was no way he could get out of it before it did.

'The only chance is that the rats aren't hungry,' he murmured to himself, but he could see that the biggest of them – a large black rat – had already begun to gnaw away on the rope as if there were no tomorrow – which, as far as Nicobobinus could see, was exactly the situation.

'Rope's bad for you!' he shouted at the rat. 'It'll tie your inside in knots!' But the big black rat took no notice of his advice, and the smaller brown rats, who had only been sniffing around the loose strands up till then, suddenly joined in the gnawing as if Nicobobinus's voice had been a starting pistol.

'Perhaps the best thing's not to look,' thought Nicobobinus to himself. 'I'll enjoy the view as long as I can and when I go . . . at least I'll go quickly . . .'

And he settled himself down with his back to the cliff and gazed across to the distant islands, and he thought about Rosie and wondered where *she* was, and he gazed at his golden feet that had caused so much of the trouble, and

he remembered the Golden Man and the dreadful Dr Sebastian and even the name Basilcat drifted into his mind, although he was certain he had never come across anyone of that name ... And the sun beat down, and the waves below him crashed against the foot of the cliff, and the rats gnawed and gnawed and gnawed ... And the first strands of the rope snapped ... and still the big rat gnawed and all the brown rats gnawed ... and another strand snapped, and the heavy iron cage jolted ... And Nicobobinus closed his eyes and thought about other things and other places ...

'I wonder if there *is* a God?' he thought to himself. 'I suppose there must be ... in any case I can't see why in the world there shouldn't be ... The only real question is ... what's he like?'

And, if you had asked Nicobobinus's opinion about God at that precise moment, as the cage shuddered a second time and yet another strand of rope snapped and the rope began to give, I'm afraid he wouldn't have been able to give you a very high opinion of him. 'Not if the Abbot and that lot are anything to go by,' he thought to himself, and the rope above started unravelling faster and faster ...

A few seconds later, Nicobobinus had completely changed his mind about God, for as the last fibres finally snapped, and the iron cage began to plummet down towards the deep green sea, a most incredible thing happened. From round the headland formed by the cliff, there suddenly swept a great black ship in full sail, and its sails scooped the cage out of the air as it fell, and then shot it down the shrouds and across the deck until the cage skidded with a great crash against the quarter-deck.

And *that* was the moment at which Rosie woke up!

15

Stuff and Rabbits!

Rosie screamed with fright, for there was a most terrific crash, against the side of the Captain's cabin, where she had been sleeping. A wooden chest and a heavy bunch of keys fell off the shelf above her and just missed her head as she sat bolt upright in the Captain's bed.

'I'm dreaming!' she said, because there in front of her, grinning at her through the quarter-deck window, was a face that, she could almost swear, belonged to her best friend, Nicobobinus.

Rosie was up out of bed in no time, and tugging at the door of Nicobobinus's cage, before he'd even had time to get his breath back.

'What an amazing bit of luck!' he said, when he could speak.

'Don't you believe it!' replied Rosie, and described to Nicobobinus everything that had happened the previous night.

Then Nicobobinus described to Rosie everything that had happened to him in the land of the Uskoks. 'But however magic this ship is,' he finished, 'it's *not* going to be able to get me out of this cage.'

'No,' replied Rosie, and the great ship rolled as if in agreement. Then it rolled again. And again.

'What's happening?' exclaimed Nicobobinus, as the cage started sliding across the deck. 'It's trying to chuck me in the sea.'

'No it isn't!' cried Rosie, 'it's shaking its head!'

'What?' said Nicobobinus.

'I'm sure it is . . . It's saying . . . Wait a minute! I know what it's saying! What a noodle!' And she disappeared into the door to the Captain's cabin. A few seconds later she reappeared, grinning all over her face and holding up the bunch of keys.

'It nearly dropped these on my head when you arrived!' she said, and she proceeded to try them in the three padlocks on Nicobobinus's cage. It was almost no surprise at all to Rosie that the first three keys she tried fitted perfectly, and Nicobobinus was soon out of the cage and giving her a big hug.

'Right!' he said. 'Now let's find the Land of Dragons. Being made of gold is a pain in the neck, hand and feet . . . I need *Dragons' Blood*!'

Down by the tiller, they found the twig still floating in the bowl of water. It showed that the boat was now sailing west. So Rosie and Nicobobinus both leant on the great beam of wood to turn the ship around.

'That's funny,' said Nicobobinus, after they had been struggling a few moments. 'D'you remember last time – before those so-called monks attacked us – the tiller just turned of its own accord . . .'

'Maybe it doesn't want us to turn around,' murmured Rosie.

But eventually they got the tiller to move, and they felt the great ship turning.

'We'd better re-set the sails or something,' said Nicobobinus, and he sprinted up onto the deck, and Rosie followed.

But when they got there they realised they didn't know which ropes to slacken off and which to haul in or anything. And as they were puzzling as to what to do, they felt the ship turning once again. By the time they had run back to the tiller, they found they were once again set on a westerly course.

'Look, ship!' shouted Rosie, 'My friend's got to get to the Land of Dragons. He needs some Dragons' blood! He's got to get cured!'

But the ship just sailed on.

Nicobobinus grabbed the tiller once again, and struggled and strained.

'I'm going east to the Land of Dragons!' he cried. 'Whether you like it or not!' And with that he pushed and heaved, and eventually he got it round, and when they were finally heading east once more, he lashed the tiller so that it wouldn't change course again. And then they went back on deck to work out the sails.

But the moment they got on deck, they felt the ship turning yet again. 'I don't believe it!' exclaimed Nicobobinus.

Rosie stamped her foot: 'Stop it, Black Ship!' she yelled. 'Stop it this minute!' But the ship just kept on turning, and when Nicobobinus got to the tiller he found that the ropes, with which he'd secured it, had snapped as if they were cotton threads, and the ship was sailing on oblivious on her westerly course.

Rosie looked at Nicobobinus. And Nicobobinus looked at Rosie.

'It really doesn't want us to go to the Land of Dragons,' said Rosie.

'Stuff and rabbits!' said Nicobobinus, and he pushed on the tiller once again, and this time, once the ship was heading east he nailed the tiller in place.

But as soon as they got up on deck, they felt the great ship turning yet again. And no matter what they did, they simply could not change the mysterious Black Ship from its westerly course.

'It's got a mind of its own,' observed Rosie.

'It beats me,' said Nicobobinus, and he slumped exhausted onto the bed in the Captain's cabin.

'But why does it want us to go west?' complained Rosie.

'Maybe we'll find out sooner or later,' said Nicobobinus, shutting his eyes, and they did.

16

Rosie's Great Discovery

It was Rosie who found it.

'I've found it!' she said.

'You've found it?' said Nicobobinus.

'Yes,' said Rosie. 'I've found it.'

'Great!' said Nicobobinus. 'I'm glad.' Then there was a bit of a pause while Rosie did a little dance of pleasure. Then Nicobobinus said: 'Rosie, I haven't the slightest idea what you're talking about.'

'*It*!' laughed Rosie. 'The *reason* the ship won't go east!'

This is what had happened. While Nicobobinus had been lying on the captain's bed, Rosie had decided to examine the other thing that had nearly dropped on her head. It was a stout wooden chest with a heavy iron clasp. 'That would certainly have hurt a lot,' thought Rosie, 'if I hadn't woken up.' However, she got the bunch of keys again and the fourth key that Rosie tried fitted the lock. Rosie had been half-hoping that chest would contain treasure – diamonds or golden doubloons or something of that sort – but it didn't.

What it did contain, however, was certainly the next best thing as far as Rosie was concerned - it was a map.

'Maybe there's an X to mark the spot where the treasure's buried', thought Rosie. But there wasn't a single X anywhere on the chart. It did, however, contain something which, believe it or not, was even more exciting to Rosie than treasure.

'I've found it!' exclaimed Rosie - and then there followed the conversation you have just heard.

Rosie and Nicobobinus spread the chart out on the floor of the Captain's cabin. It was very old and it showed a part of the world that Nicobobinus had never seen before.

'Look!' cried Rosie - very excited - 'Look! Do you see where we're heading?'

Nicobobinus looked, and he got a very funny feeling

inside his tummy – it was a bit like drinking a cup of cool, clear mountain water, on a hot, dusty day, and then remembering you'd put your pet fish in it.

He followed Rosie's finger as she traced the Black Ship's westerly course, further and further into the unknown waters beyond the world they knew, beyond the world of any map they had ever seen, until they came to a strange land . . . at least they *thought* it was land, but they weren't absolutely positive, for there on the shore were written the following words: 'Here lies the Ocean of Mountains'.

'Well, which is it?' demanded Nicobobinus, 'Mountains or Ocean?'

'But look here!' cried Rosie, and Nicobobinus looked beyond and read: 'Here lies the City of Cries'.

'And there! There!' cried Rosie, and Nicobobinus looked even further, deep into that strange and somehow sinister realm (for even on the map it looked somehow threatening), and there he read the words that had got Rosie so excited: 'Here lies the Land of Dragons'!

17

The Ocean of Mountains

Rosie and Nicobobinus sailed on through the seas for day after day. They found food and water in the galley whenever they wanted it, they slept in the Captain's cabin snug and warm. The sun shone and the sea was calm, and at night the stars above them seemed to urge them on deeper and deeper into unknown waters.

One morning, however, Nicobobinus woke up, looked down at his feet, and cried out: 'Rosie! I'm cured!'

Rosie leapt out of bed and stared at Nicobobinus's smiling face, and then down at his feet.

'No you're not,' she said.

'Well ... no ...' agreed Nicobobinus. 'I just felt like saying it, because ... ' But he never finished the sentence, for he was staring out of the cabin window. Rosie followed his gaze and then caught her breath, for there outside was a sandy shore with mountains in the distance.

'We're there!' she breathed, 'Wherever it is ... '

'According to the chart, this should be the Ocean of Mountains,' said Nicobobinus, as he and Rosie waded ashore.

'And the Land of Dragons lies on the other side,' said Rosie, peering over his shoulder.

They both stood there, with their feet sinking into the sand, and their hearts sinking into their boots.

'It looks a bloomin' long way,' said Rosie.

And Nicobobinus agreed: 'How are we going to do it?' he asked.

'I suppose we start walking,' said Rosie.

'But we ought to take provisions and so on,' said Nicobobinus.

'Oh come on!' said Rosie, 'Let's just go!'

'No! Let's work it out!' said Nicobobinus – very sensibly, I think.

So they sat and argued about when to set off and what to take, and although I don't think Rosie was being very sensible, in this instance, it was she who won the argument ... or, rather, it was the ship that resolved the argument for her.

As they were drawing maps in the sand, Rosie happened to glance over her shoulder. 'NICO!' she cried. And Nicobobinus turned to see the Black Ship had weighed anchor and was now sailing away towards the horizon.

'Stop! Come back!' they cried and they both waded into the sea to swim after the ship. But the sails had caught the wind, and besides, Nicobobinus and Rosie could see sharks' fins cutting the waters between them and the ship. Hastily they struggled back onto the shore, and stared, as their only link with the world they knew disappeared from sight.

Nicobobinus looked at Rosie in despair, and the moment he saw what she was doing he became very indignant. You may have guessed what Rosie was doing ... she was grinning all over her face.

'Rosie!' said Nicobobinus. 'Did I ever tell you you were a looney?'

'It's just that I hate arguing with you,' said Rosie, 'and now I don't have to . . .' And she turned, and started walking towards the mountains.

'Rosie!' cried Nicobobinus. 'I'll never make it!'

'*Nicobobinus*!' exclaimed Rosie. 'Don't you remember? You can do *anything*!'

And that was how Rosie and Nicobobinus came to one of the most amazing places in the world - or even out of it - the Ocean of Mountains.

'It's so much steeper here than it looked from the beach,' said Nicobobinus.

Rosie didn't reply. She was finding it hard going too, and she was wondering how long Nicobobinus would be able to keep going with his heavy feet.

'Still, it can't be that far to the top of this first hill,' said Nicobobinus to cheer her up, 'and then it'll be downhill for a bit.'

'Then there's that big mountain further on . . . ' thought Rosie to herself, but she didn't say it.

So they kept on climbing, and by the time night fell, they were still climbing.

They were both hungry and thirsty, but as they hadn't brought any stores with them from the ship, there was nothing else for it but to curl up together for warmth and try to sleep.

When dawn broke, they were cold and fed up. And when Rosie looked up the mountainside, she was even more fed up.

'I don't believe it!' she cried. 'It's as if we just hadn't got anywhere.'

Nicobobinus looked too, and agreed. It looked as if they were back where they had started, and yet there was something different about it all . . .

'It's as if the hill we spent all yesterday climbing had never existed!' thought Nicobobinus, but he said: 'Come on! Let's get going!' And they began the long uphill slog.

And they climbed and they climbed all that day. And they got hungrier and colder and more and more exhausted – especially Nicobobinus who could hardly drag his heavy feet uphill with him as he climbed.

Eventually the sun began to set, and they were still only half-way up the mountain, with a long gruelling climb ahead of them. But in the last red rays of the sun, they saw something that gave them hope.

'Do you see, Nico?' said Rosie excitedly. 'Beyond the top of the mountain?'

'That cloud?' asked Nicobobinus.

'It's not a cloud! It's smoke!' cried Rosie.

'And where there's smoke there's usually people,' smiled Nicobobinus, and the two of them curled up, determined to get to the top of the mountain the next day.

But when dawn broke, they both had a nasty shock.

It was Nicobobinus who woke up first, and he thought he must be still dreaming. While he was rubbing his eyes, Rosie woke up too, and she took one look at Nicobobinus and said something so rude that if I were to write it down, I'm sure it would burn a hole in the paper.

'Am I *really* going mad?' asked Nicobobinus, 'Or did we go to sleep last night half-way up this mountain?'

Rosie's reply was even ruder than what she had said before. But there was no getting away from it. Wherever they had fallen asleep last night, this morning they were well and truly at the bottom of the mountain.

'It's not fair!' cried Rosie. 'We climbed and climbed all day, and now we've got to start all over again!'

At this point, I have to tell you that Rosie - not unreasonably in my opinion - burst into tears. Nicobobinus half wished he had done it first, because that's just what he felt like doing too. However, since Rosie had started, he decided he had to cheer her up.

'Look!' he said, jumping to his feet with a cheeriness he did not feel. 'I don't know what's happened. Maybe we got blown back down in the night. Or maybe we were just magicked back. But whatever it was, we can't stay here. And I'm not going back. Let's climb and see what happens today.'

Rosie really agreed with everything Nicobobinus had just said, so they began the long climb.

The way seemed even steeper and harder than before, and Nicobobinus grew more and more exhausted.

'If he doesn't get a square meal soon,' thought Rosie, 'he's going to peg out!'

At lunchtime, however (or, rather, what would have been lunchtime if they had had any lunch to lunch off), they discovered a mountain pool, and they were at least able to drink. Rosie went for a swim, while Nicobobinus looked on enviously.

'I'll never make it!' he wanted to say. But he didn't, and after 'lunch' they set off again, up and up. And the way grew steeper and Rosie grew tired, and Nicobobinus kept having to rest, and Rosie thought: 'We'll never make it.'

And some time later Nicobobinus *said*: 'I'll never make it,' and then he slumped down on a rock, as evening closed around them. After a moment, however, Rosie nudged Nicobobinus. 'Look!' she said.

Nicobobinus raised his weary eyes towards the summit that still seemed as far off as ever. There was a plume of smoke rising from the mountainside a few hundred feet above them.

'That's odd ... ' said Nicobobinus. 'Yesterday the smoke was the *other* side of the mountain.'

'Who cares!' cried Rosie, scrambling to her feet. 'I'm hungry! Come on!' And she started scrambling up the rocky slope as fast as she could, and Nicobobinus struggled on behind.

Night closed around them as they ran up the mountain, but now they could see a light burning from where the smoke had been coming from, and they knew there must be someone sitting over a warm fire, cooking some supper.

'And who knows?' panted Rosie, 'they'll probably be really pleased to get visitors!'

At that moment, however, the light went out.

'Bother!' thought Rosie. 'They've gone to bed!'

But they struggled on uphill, tripping and stumbling in the moonlight, until they finally reached a curious little log cabin that looked somehow like a boat only not quite ... From the cabin the sound of snoring rose with great clarity and vigour.

Nicobobinus collapsed in an exhausted golden heap, while Rosie screwed up her courage and rapped sharply on the door of the cabin.

The snoring paused for a brief moment, as if considering the interruption, and then carried on with renewed vigour.

Rosie knocked again. But the snoring went on ... and on ... and on ...

No matter how hard she knocked, nor how loud she shouted in at the window, nothing - it seemed - could wake the sleeper up.

Rosie and Nicobobinus, however, were desperate.

'Come on!' said Rosie. 'If he doesn't wake up with that racket, he won't wake up if we go in and get something to eat.' For, to tell the truth, they could smell a delicious stew that was still simmering over the embers.

Very cautiously, Rosie pushed the door open. The snoring was almost deafening.

Feeling around in the darkness, she found a lantern, and they soon had it alight with a glowing piece of wood from the fire.

The room that the lantern now lit up was a curious one in many respects. But, without a shadow of doubt, by far the most curious thing about it was the Snorer.

He was a little goblin of a man with red cheeks and red whiskers and a red night cap, all of which shook and trembled as he snored. But quite the most remarkable thing about him was the fact that he was sitting bolt upright in his bed, with his eyes wide open, watching them!

18

The Snorer

Rosie nearly jumped out of her skin and Nicobobinus hid behind the door.

'Oh! I'm sorry!' cried Rosie. 'I thought you were asleep.'

The strange little man shrugged his shoulders: 'Asleep or awake – it's all the same to me,' he said and carried on snoring as loudly as before with his eyes still wide open watching them.

'May . . . may we come in?' asked Rosie nervously.

'Looks to me as if you *are* in,' observed the Snoring Man.

'Yes . . . ' said Rosie looking round, 'I'm sorry. Is it all right?'

'Out or in – what's the difference?' sighed the little man.

'Well it makes a difference to us,' ventured Nicobobinus. 'Because we're cold and tired and we've been climbing all day.'

'Well more fool you,' said the little man. 'Why don't you wait? That's what I do.'

'Well you see ... ' Nicobobinus wasn't quite sure what they were talking about, but he carried on anyway, 'you see ... we're in a hurry, and ... '

'Never any good being in a hurry,' said the man, and went on snoring.

'Well we're not in a *hurry* exactly ... ' said Nicobobinus.

'May we have some food?' cut in Rosie, who couldn't see what they were talking about either. 'We haven't eaten for three days.'

'Stew's always ready,' said the little man, and so without another word Rosie and Nicobobinus helped themselves, while the Snorer carried on snoring as loud as ever, but with his eyes wide open, watching them.

When they had finished they sat and looked at the man for some time, and he sat, bolt upright in bed, snoring and looking at them. Eventually Nicobobinus said:

'Excuse me. I know it's an odd question but are you asleep or awake?'

'Makes no difference to me,' said the Snoring Man. 'I can do both at once. What are your names?'

Nicobobinus and Rosie had to shout their names to make themselves heard above the snoring. Then the man grunted and said:

'My name's Loris ... Captain Loris ... Sorry, I'm sleeping rather heavily at the moment.' And, indeed, his snores seemed to be louder than ever. 'But welcome aboard anyway,' he added.

'Is this a boat?' asked Nicobobinus.

'Well sort of ... ' replied Captain Loris. 'It's a mountain boat.'

'Oh ... I see,' said Nicobobinus, while Rosie thought to herself: 'What nonsense! I've never heard of such a thing!'

'*Aaaarrgh*!' cried Captain Loris, suddenly. And both Rosie and Nicobobinus leapt out of their seats. 'Sorry ... having a nightmare ... Terrible dream about evil monks.'

'Evil monks?' exclaimed Nicobobinus ... 'I know them!'

'Not these!' said Captain Loris. 'These monks were pirates. That sort of thing only happens in dreams.'

'But pirate monks *did* capture our boat and they did try to kill Nicobobinus!' said Rosie.

'No no ... I told you - it was only a dream,' said Captain Loris.

'But it actually happened!' said Nicobobinus.

'And they were going to starve him to death and then cut off his feet and hand!' cried Rosie.

'But the worst bit,' said Captain Loris, 'was when they hung him in a cage over the sea with rats gnawing the ropes.'

'How did you know about that?' exclaimed Nicobob-inus.

'Because it was all part of the dream, of course!' said Captain Loris.

'But it was real!' insisted Nicobobinus.

'No no – you really must learn to distinguish between dreams and reality, young man, or you'll find life forever an uphill struggle.'

'Well it's certainly that at the moment,' said Rosie.

'That's because you've been *trying* to go uphill!' cried the odd little man. 'I can't for the life of me understand why you don't try going *downhill*!'

Rosie and Nicobobinus looked at each other.

'Well . . . er . . . we . . . well we want to get to the Land of Dragons,' said Rosie.

Captain Loris suddenly stopped snoring and said: 'Bother! I just woke up! Do you mind speaking a bit more softly?'

'Oh . . . sorry,' whispered Rosie.

'Sorry . . . ' whispered Nicobobinus.

'The Land of Dragons?' said the Captain. 'Now that's a nightmare . . . no place for children.'

'But we have to go there!' cried Rosie. 'We've got to get some dragon's blood to cure Nicobobinus.' And Nicobobinus held up his golden hand.

Captain Loris bent across and tapped it, and then looked at Nicobobinus very hard. 'You're sure you're not dreaming that?'

'I wish I were,' said Nicobobinus, 'but you wouldn't be able to see or touch it, if it were just my dream.'

'Ah!' said Captain Loris. 'But *I* might be a part of the dream too . . . '

Rosie couldn't see where all this was leading, so she

said: 'Anyway, we've got to cross these mountains to get to the Land of Dragons.'

'But that doesn't mean you have to go *up* them,' sighed the little old man.

'Well how else are we going to cross them?' demanded Rosie who was getting a bit irritable, if the truth were told.

'Now my dear young people,' said Captain Loris, getting off the bed and helping himself to a bit of stew, 'you don't seem to know where you are.'

'Yes we do!' said Nicobobinus. 'This is the Ocean of Mountains.'

'Exactly!' said Captain Loris. 'It's an ocean . . . these mountains are just waves – they're going up and down all the time.'

'You mean . . . these mountains are *moving*!' exclaimed Rosie.

'Of course,' said the Captain. 'Naturally they move very, very slowly because . . . well . . . rock is slower than water. But they're moving all the same. The valleys are going up and the mountains are going down just like any other ocean.'

Suddenly a light came into Rosie's eyes: 'Then all we've got to do,' she said, 'is stay put, and we'll eventually find ourselves on *top* of a mountain?'

'Exactly. *Then* you can start walking down, and it'll be downhill all the way. It's a bit like surfing,' said the Captain.

'What's *surfing*?' asked Nicobobinus.

'Oh just something I once dreamed about,' replied Captain Loris. 'Oh good! I've fallen asleep again. Look why don't we *all* turn in, and see where we are in the morning?'

And that's what they did.

19

The Wall Across the World

The next day broke bright and clear over the Ocean of Mountains. Nicobobinus and Rosie found that Captain Loris's cabin (or as he insisted on calling it, mountain boat) was down in a valley. So instead of setting off, they helped him cut firewood, and get his home ship-shape. And by lunchtime, they found they were on top of a mountain again. They quickly ate some more stew, filled a pot with the left-overs, and set off down the mountainside towards the Land of Dragons.

'But don't forget!' called Captain Loris after them, 'Don't go too fast or you'll find yourselves going uphill again. Remember this is an ocean - you can only go at the ocean's speed.'

And the sound of his snoring accompanied them until they were almost halfway down. There they stopped, and rested, and ate a little stew, and talked, and picked wild mountain flowers, and they saw the sun beginning to set. By now they realised they were on the crest of a mountain again. So they ran down to the very bottom, and made a camp there in the valley for the night.

By daybreak, they were once again on the very peak of a mountain, and they were able to set off downhill once more.

In this manner, taking their time, without hurrying, and without once having to go uphill, they crossed the Ocean of Mountains in a few days.

'And to think,' said Rosie, 'if we hadn't met that funny little man, we would probably have died of exhaustion by now!'

'Life is full of mysteries,' murmured Nicobobinus, and – once again – the name 'Basilcat' popped into his mind, though he couldn't think why.

When they had crossed the Ocean of Mountains they found themselves crossing a vast desert plain, like a dried up sea. There was nothing but rock and dust wasting away, with, every now and then, huge dried-up leaves like seaweed, that had gone brown as the dust and yet were soft like fine silk, and which lay there billowing out in the hot breeze.

Nicobobinus and Rosie journeyed on, under the baking sun, until Nicobobinus suddenly stopped, and screwed up his eyes.

'What's that on the horizon?' he said.

Rosie couldn't make it out either. So they travelled on for some time, and, to their surprise, they found the horizon getting nearer.

'That's funny,' said Rosie, 'the horizon usually stays where it is.'

'Maybe it's the Edge of the World,' said Nicobobinus.

'Don't be daft!' replied Rosie. 'The World doesn't have an edge – it's round. Didn't you know?'

'Of course I did,' said Nicobobinus (although I'm not at all sure that he *did*). But still the horizon got nearer and nearer – just as if it *were* the Edge of the World – until Nicobobinus suddenly exclaimed: 'It can't be!'

'What?' said Rosie.

'It's a ... I can't believe it ...' said Nicobobinus. 'It's not possible!'

But it was!

As I sit here writing this down, looking out of my window over the roof tops of London, it still seems scarcely credible, and yet there it was! Right in front of them ...

'It's a wall!' exclaimed Rosie.

And indeed it was. It stretched from horizon to horizon, cutting them off from the entire world beyond.

'This whole adventure began with a wall,' said Nicobobinus, 'and now it looks as if it's going to end with one – a wall across the world!'

And, indeed, even Rosie found herself agreeing.

'Even if I stood on your shoulders again,' said Nicobobinus, 'I wouldn't be able to reach even half-way up this wall.'

'There must be a door or something!' said Rosie. 'Come on!'

And they set off walking along the bottom of the vast wall, walking and walking, hoping every minute that they would see a break in the solid stonework. But they didn't.

They walked and walked, and the sun beat down, but they came across not a window, not a gatehouse, not a door ... only the unyielding stone wall.

'This is ridiculous!' said Rosie at last, sitting down on a rock. 'There *must* be a way in.'

'Beats me,' said Nicobobinus, and he stretched himself out on the ground.

Rosie stamped her feet in frustration. 'It can't end like

this!' she said. 'Not after all we've been through ... You can't have a story that just ends with us coming to a stone wall and having to turn round and go home again!'

'If this were a story,' said Nicobobinus, in a dreamy sort of way, 'we'd get over somehow. Maybe we'd pile all the rocks and stones into a heap until we could reach the top ... or we'd meet a little man who would tell us the magic words to say so we could fly over ...' But he broke off, and opened one eye to look at Rosie.

She was already piling the rocks and stones into a heap against the wall.

'Nicobobinus! You're a genius!' said Rosie.

'Rosie!' said Nicobobinus. 'You're a looncy! We'll never make a pile big enough!'

'We can do it!' said Rosie cheerfully, and they both set to work.

Some time later they had a pile that reached about up to Rosie's shoulder, but the higher it got the more difficult it became and the more the stones and rocks kept slipping down and the pile would collapse.

'What was the other idea you had?' asked Rosie eventually.

'Er ... a little man telling us the magic words so that we could fly over,' said Nicobobinus.

'Let's keep piling up the stones,' said Rosie, and she redoubled her efforts, and Nicobobinus had to work hard to keep up with her.

By nightfall they had a pile as high as Rosie's head. So they wrapped themselves in one of the soft seaweed-like leaves, and slept soundly.

By the end of the next day, they had a pile as high as Nicobobinus's head.

'It's still not enough,' moaned Rosie.

'Maybe tomorrow we . . .' said Nicobobinus sleepily.

It was at that moment that they noticed a face looking down at them from over the top of the wall.

'Oh!' exclaimed Rosie.

'Ah!' said Nicobobinus.

'What do you two think you're doing?' demanded the soldier.

'We want to get over the wall,' said Rosie.

'Well you can't!' said the soldier. 'It's illegal!'

'Well is there a gate or a door we can go through?' asked Nicobobinus.

'No!' said the man. 'We don't want anyone coming in. Now go away or I'll shoot.'

And they suddenly realised that he was aiming a cross-bow right at Nicobobinus's head.

'I think those were the magic words . . .' muttered Rosie to Nicobobinus.

'Go on!' said the man. 'Go home before the White Wind comes!' and he put his finger on the catch of his crossbow.

'You're wrong, Rosie!' said Nicobobinus under his breath, as they pretended to walk away. '*Those* were the magic words.'

'What are you talking about?' said Rosie.

'Wait and see,' said Nicobobinus.

When they got far enough away from the soldier on the wall, they hid under a seaweed leaf and waited for him to stop looking.

Time passed and the breezes blew hotter and stronger, and dark clouds began racing across the sun, and it was all Nicobobinus and Rosie could do to keep themselves covered.

But at last they saw the soldier's head disappear back behind the wall, as the wind blew the dust up into suffocating clouds that turned everything white.

'This is it!' breathed Nicobobinus. 'The White Wind.'

'I'm frightened,' said Rosie. And in my opinion she was right – for there was a terrible power in the way the wind was rising . . . in the way it hurled the dust against the stone wall and in the way it tore at the seaweed shroud that covered them.

'Hang on!' said Nicobobinus as they began to feel the billowing folds of seaweed leaf dragging them across the rocky floor, and the wind roared.

'Ow!' cried Rosie as she hit a rock, and the white wind blew stronger and the leaf dragged them faster and faster across the plain, and the dust clouds blotted out the sun.

'Can you feel it?' yelled Nicobobinus. 'The White Wind! Those were the magic words . . . and now . . .'

Rosie felt herself being lifted up by the fury of the wind . . .

'We're going to fly!' cried Nicobobinus, and up they went! Faster and faster the wind blew, and the silken leaf mushroomed as it caught the white wind and pulled them up, clear of the rocky ground, and pulled them higher and higher up through the dust cloud . . .

'We'll hit the wall!' cried Rosie. 'We'll be smashed to bits!'

'Hang on!' cried Nicobobinus.

And up they went, higher and higher, riding the White Wind that blew with all its might across that barren plain. And where it hit the wall it shot up towards the sky, carrying Rosie and Nicobobinus with it, until they found themselves parachuting gently down, on the other side of the impenetrable stone wall.

'You know,' said Rosie, after they'd got their breath back, 'there are times when I think this is all just a story . . .'

'Listen!' said Nicobobinus. 'Do you hear? We must be in the City of Cries!'

20

The City of Cries

After the howling of the wind had died away and the dust storm had blown itself out, Nicobobinus and Rosie looked about them.

They found they had landed in the courtyard of a magnificent house. The walls were clad in white marble, and the ground was paved with rich mosaics worked in blue and red and silver leaf. In the middle of the courtyard, fountains played – each one sending up a plume of water of a different colour.

'I thought Venice was a fine city,' whispered Nicobobinus, 'but this place is a real holiday for the eyeballs!'

The words were hardly out of his mouth, however, when a window behind them opened and a small voice said: 'Help!'

Nicobobinus and Rosie saw a pale, sad-faced child beckoning to them urgently.

'Please hurry!' cried the child, and there was such a note of terror in her voice that both Rosie and Nicobobinus leapt to their feet. But before they could move, they saw a soldier grab the little girl and slam the shutter. They heard a muffled cry, and then all was quiet again, save for the distant moans and shrieks of countless unseen souls that forever filled the air. When they ran to the window, there was no sign of either the child or the soldier.

Rosie and Nicobobinus looked at each other.

'Uh-oh!' said Rosie. 'Let's get out of here!'

'But which way?' asked Nicobobinus.

'In situations like this, my dad always says there's only one way to go!' said Rosie.

'Which way's that?' asked Nicobobinus.

'Fast,' said Rosie, and she raced for the nearest door. Nicobobinus joined her, and they were busy pulling back the great bolts that held it, when they noticed they were being watched . . . by three guards armed with swords and pikes.

'Uh-oh . . .' said Rosie.

'Oh-uh . . .' said Nicobobinus.

'Grab 'em,' said the chief guard.

When they had been grabbed, the chief guard looked them over.

'Names?' he said.

Nicobobinus and Rosie gave the only names they had.

'Numbers?' snapped the chief guard.

'Er . . . what do you mean?' asked Nicobobinus.

'He wants to know your number,' said one of the other guards.

'Well . . . there's two of us?' ventured Rosie.

'No no! Numbers for identification,' said the helpful guard.

'We haven't got any,' said Nicobobinus.

The Chief Guard looked as if he were about to explode in a ball of flame. The helpful guard stared at him anxiously, and then whispered to Nicobobinus:

'You must have a number . . . Say anything for now!'

'2 . . . 4 . . . 3 . . . 9,' said Nicobobinus.

'Er . . . 1 . . . 5 . . . 8 . . . 9!' said Rosie. '7,6,5,4,3,2,1 . . . Zero!'

'Don't overdo it!' whispered Nicobobinus.

The Chief Guard's colour returned to normal and he jotted these numbers down.

'Method of entry?' he barked.

'How did you get in?' whispered the helpful guard.

'We came on the wind,' said Rosie.

'Oh dear!' muttered the helpful guard, and then he turned to the Chief Guard who was turning bright red again, and said:

'They say they climbed in, sir!'

'Right!' snapped the Chief Guard. 'Tower cell for the girl! Deep dungeon for the boy!'

'Er . . . Hugo . . .' said the third guard, tapping the leader on the shoulder.

'Chains and no lights for the rest of their lives!' rapped out the Chief Guard, turning on his heel.

'Er . . . Hugo!' said the third guard again, tugging the leader's sleeve. 'Have you looked at the boy's feet?'

The Chief Guard turned round very slowly and stared at Nicobobinus's feet.

And suddenly Rosie and Nicobobinus found themselves being marched into the grand house, through room after magnificent room, until they came to a pair of ornate doors. Here the Chief Guard rapped three times.

A voice said: 'Enter,' and they marched in to a very splendid audience chamber.

There were crowds of people in the room, murmuring together in huddles, bowing and backing and waving rolls of parchment.

Sitting on a throne at the far end was a thin white-haired old man.

'Found these two intruders in the Fountain Court,' announced the Chief Guard.

'Well don't bother *me* with them!' exclaimed the white-haired old man. 'Throw them in the dungeons, Hugo! I'm in the middle of giving an audience.'

'Yes ... normally ... of course ...' said the Chief Guard. 'But the boy's made of *gold*!'

Suddenly the entire room fell silent. All eyes - including the watery blue eyes of the white-haired old man - focussed on Nicobobinus.

'Come here, boy,' commanded the old man. He looked at Nicobobinus, then he called out: 'Jeweller!'

A man in a gown hurried forward and examined Nicobobinus's hand and feet. Then he turned to the old man, and bowed. 'Gold, your majesty,' he said.

All at once everyone in the room started whispering to everyone else, in great excitement.

The old man leant back in his throne and smiled a broad smile.

'Well ... well ... my boy ... You must be tired? Take a seat ... Steward! Bring some food and drink ... you *are* hungry, aren't you? ... This is indeed an honour ...'

'Er ... Your majesty!' interrupted the Chief Guard. 'Shall I throw the girl in the tower cell with chains and no lights for the rest of her life?'

'She hasn't any ... er ...' said the old man.

'No, your majesty,' replied the guard.

Suddenly Nicobobinus found his voice: 'She's my very dear friend!' he said loud and clear.

The old King paused. He looked from one to the other.

'I look after him,' added Rosie for good measure.

The King smiled. 'Then you are both welcome to the City of Silence,' he said, and dismissed the entire court with a clap of his hands.

'We thought this was the City of Cries?' said Rosie.

'Wherever did you get that idea?' asked the King.

'Well it's on our chart,' said Nicobobinus. 'And in any case ... listen!'

The King listened for a few seconds and then beamed: 'Beautiful isn't it?'

'No it isn't,' said Rosie. 'It's bloodcurdling!'

'Ah ... not everyone can stand such absolute silence to begin with,' said the King. 'But you'll soon get used to it. And now let's introduce ourselves. I am King Pactolus. Lord of the City of Silence.'

21

King Pactolus

King Pactolus turned out to be a very affectionate man. He treated everyone with equal care and consideration – even if they were not actually the richest in the land, as long as they had wealth or fame or power, all his subjects were equally dear to him.

Nicobobinus found himself particularly welcome. The King gave up one of his own thirty or forty personal bedrooms for him to use, and Rosie was given the room next door.

But in spite of all this neither Nicobobinus nor Rosie felt very happy at all.

They never forgot the frightened face of the child they had seen when they had first arrived, and they never got used to the continual background of cries and moans that filled the air.

'This place gives me the creeps!' said Rosie.

'I agree,' said Nicobobinus. 'I don't trust this King Pactolus further than I can throw a chicken bone.'

'He's after your gold – as sure as I'm not Dutch!' said Rosie.

But the King continued to shower them with every kindness and somehow made it impossible for them ever to leave.

'We must be going, King Pactolus!' Rosie would say, as they drank wine for breakfast. 'We've got to get to the Land of Dragons!'

'Plenty of time, my dears,' the King would reply with a wave of his hand, and a servant would bring up a silver dish with yet another roast pheasant on it.

Rosie and Nicobobinus, however, began to find they no longer had the will to eat. And, despite the feasts and banquets and scandalous breakfasts, they began to grow thin and pale . . . just like King Pactolus himself.

One day Rosie said: 'This has gone on long enough! Look at you, Nicobobinus! If we don't get out of here soon, we'll be coffin-cases!' And the two of them packed some things in a bag and marched down to the main doors of the Palace. But the guard blocked their way.

'Sorry,' he said, 'King Pactolus's orders.'

'Come on, Nico,' said Rosie, 'let's go back to our room.' And they went round to one of the state chambers at the side, and climbed out of a window.

But no sooner had they set foot on the street than there was a shout from a guard on the roof.

'Run!' cried Rosie.

But they were both weak, and Nicobobinus fell over his heavy gold feet. Rosie helped him up, and they staggered across the road as the guards came pouring out of the Palace.

'Down here!' said Rosie, and they dodged down an alley-way. But the guards were after them, pushing aside the ragged townspeople, who filled the streets. And before

Rosie and Nicobobinus were halfway down the alley, an old pile of rags suddenly stuck out his foot, and they both tripped and went sprawling in the gutter. And the guards had surrounded them and marched them back to the Palace before they could say: 'Hey! Let go!'

Back in the Palace, King Pactolus looked very grave.

'My dear children,' he said, 'it is for your own safety that I am concerned. You saw how the streets are crowded with ruffians and paupers. I'm afraid Nicobobinus would not last half an hour out there. Have some roast suckling pig.'

And after that Rosie and Nicobobinus found there was someone watching them, ready to raise the alarm, wherever they went.

Only at night were they on their own, and even then a guard would look in every hour to check they were still there.

And always the air was filled with distant cries and moans, that came and went with the wind.

And whenever Rosie and Nicobobinus asked about them, people would shrug and say: 'What cries?' or 'I can't hear anything.'

Meanwhile the days grew shorter, and the winter set in, and snow began to fall upon the City. But King Pactolus's Palace stayed warm and bright. Torches that never seemed to die out or need replacing blazed on the walls by day and by night. And the marble floors were warm to the touch even when the winds were howling across the city, and the rime-frost covered the walls, and the snow fell deep and silent.

'You know why the Palace is so warm, don't you?' said the Dwarf-Jester.

Neither Rosie nor Nicobobinus liked the Dwarf-Jester.

Not because he was a dwarf, but because he was always creeping up on you and saying out loud things that you had only just been thinking.

'No,' said Nicobobinus. 'Why?'

The Dwarf-Jester did a back-flip and landed on his feet again. Then he hit Rosie on the head with his bladder. It was this sort of behaviour that made him particularly annoying.

'You ought to find out,' he said, and jumped out of the window.

'Well he doesn't make *me* laugh,' said Rosie.

'Maybe he's trying to tell us something,' said Nicobobinus.

So the next time King Pactolus summoned them to a light snack in between breakfast and elevenses, Nicobobinus asked him how they kept the Palace so warm.

A strange glint came into King Pactolus's eyes. He put a large piece of pig's trotter into his mouth and chewed it for several minutes. Then he said: 'We will soon be moving to another Palace.'

So Nicobobinus asked him again how they kept the Palace so warm. And this time King Pactolus smiled a secret smile and said:

'Wouldn't you like to know ...' Which seemed pretty obvious in view of the question Nicobobinus had just asked.

'He doesn't want us to know!' whispered Rosie that night as they hid under Nicobobinus's bed.

'Ssh!' whispered Nicobobinus. 'There's someone coming!'

And sure enough they heard the familiar, pad, pad, pad of the guard walking towards their chamber to check they were still there.

He glanced in as usual, holding up a blazing torch. Then, having checked that Nicobobinus was safely sleeping in his bed, the guard turned away as usual, and began to pad softly away.

'He didn't notice!' whispered Rosie.

'Ssh!' said Nicobobinus, for he had just heard the guard stop. There was a pause, then the footsteps came running back to the bedroom and the guard's face appeared at the door. He had clearly just been struck by lightning.

'He's not there!' he gulped. 'He's gone!'

Then he disappeared yelling: 'The gold boy's escaped! Close the doors! Raise the alarm!'

Rosie nudged Nicobobinus. 'It worked!' she said.

'Come on!' replied Nicobobinus. 'While they're busy looking for us, we can explore.'

22

What Rosie and Nicobobinus Found Out

Nicobobinus had stolen a pair of boots to cover his golden feet, and had bound his hand with a cloth so that not a trace of gold was showing. Rosie had got hold of some servants' clothes and two buckets and two mops, and thus they were able to walk through the confusion in the Palace without anyone taking a blind bit of notice of them.

They saw King Pactolus beside himself with rage, jumping up and down on his throne in the audience chamber.

'We mustn't lose him!' the King was screaming. 'We need that gold! Winter's only just begun!'

Rosie gave Nicobobinus an 'I told you so' look, and then she said: 'I told you so! He's only after your gold.'

'But what's the winter got to do with it?' said Nicobobinus. 'Come on, let's go down here.'

They had discovered some steps that led down to the cellars. The torches were burning more dimly than usual, as they made their way down into the bowels of the Palace.

Several guards suddenly rushed up past them, looking for Nicobobinus, and shouting: 'He's not *here*!'

At the bottom of the steps, they found themselves in a maze of passageways all built of brick. There was a curious smell that Rosie had noticed before in the Palace, but it was so slight that she had got used to it. Here, however, it was much stronger, and it made them both feel rather ill.

A heavy iron door was set into one wall, and in front of it, a very pale guard was standing.

'Halt!' he said. 'You can't clean down here without permission.'

'Oh but we've got permission!' said Rosie.

'Oh ...' said the pale guard. 'But ... er ... not for in *here*!' He glanced at the door behind him.

'Oh yes! Particularly for in *there*!' said Nicobobinus.

The guard suddenly looked nervous and lowered his voice. 'But this leads to the boiler-house.'

'We know,' lied Rosie in her teeth. 'We've been ordered by King Pactolus himself to clean the boiler-house especially.'

For a moment a look of pity seemed to flash across the guard's face. Then he lowered his voice even more and said: 'It's all right. If they asks me I'll say you done it. I let you through and you done it.' And he winked an eye in a friendly sort of way.

'No ... it's very kind of you ... but we *want* to do it,' said Nicobobinus.

A look of amazement replaced the concern on the guard's face.

'You *want* to go in there?' he said.

'Yes,' said Rosie.

'But ... but ... you *know* what's in there ...' he stuttered.

'Of course,' lied Rosie again. 'So let us in – the sooner we get it done the better!'

The guard shook his head. 'You must have really upset King Pactolus,' he said, putting the great iron key into the door. Then he stopped and turned back to Rosie and Nicobobinus, and said:

'Look ... do you mind letting yourselves in? I can't bear even looking in there.'

Nicobobinus and Rosie were beginning to get a bit worried about what lay beyond the great door, but they didn't show it.

'No problem,' said Rosie.

'Thanks,' said the guard, and he sprinted off down one of the passageways and hid.

Rosie and Nicobobinus looked at each other.

'Come on!' said Nicobobinus. And – rather nervously – he began to turn the key in the lock.

Nicobobinus was so weak that it took all his strength to unlock the door, and it took the two of them to heave it open.

The first thing that struck them was the smell. The second was the noise – like a great bellows. The third thing was another door, which struck them on their noses as they walked straight into it.

'Let's take the key with us,' said Nicobobinus, as they locked the door behind them. 'Just in case . . .'

The second door was not locked, but it was massive and made of many thicknesses of iron, and Rosie and Nicobobinus had to struggle and strain as they tried to get it open. And all the time they both felt as if they had several hundred butterflies and maybe a few moths fluttering around in their stomachs, because neither of them could imagine what they would find on the other side . . .

Eventually the door creaked open, and Nicobobinus and Rosie peered in, holding their noses against the stench.

It was warm and humid as you might expect from a boiler-house, but the air was somehow stagnant. The sound of the great bellows was now accompanied by the roar of a furnace.

'This is it!' whispered Nicobobinus. 'The boiler-room that heats the Palace!'

'Oh dear!' said Rosie.

Both of them had guessed that the secret which the Dwarf-Jester had alluded to might lie behind the locked door, but neither of them had been at all prepared for the sight that now lay before them.

They found themselves on the floor of a large cellar. All about them were white-faced men, women and children. They were all clothed in the barest of rags and were as thin as sticks. Some looked half dead and they all had the dull look of horror in their eyes.

Down one side of the cellar a sheet of flame shot out from a hole in the wall almost the entire length of the room. Sometimes the flame stayed for some moments. At other times it came and went. Above the flame, huge cauldrons had been placed on a great iron frame, and the white-faced people were scurrying this way and that with buckets of water, filling the cauldrons as the flames roared.

At the far end was an archway that led into another area, the walls of which glowed red and flickered. Occasionally they saw a lick of flame and they knew that must be where the furnace was.

A pale, emaciated man glared at them.

'Well! Don't just stand there! Or we'll all get burnt up!' he said and hurried on.

So Nicobobinus and Rosie started to make their way across the room.

'Do you think this is Hell, Nicobobinus?' asked Rosie.

'If it isn't, I feel sorry for the Devil,' said Nicobobinus. 'How can that dreadful King Pactolus live in his Palace up there, eating partridges for every meal, and pheasants in between, knowing these people are living like this down here?'

Just then there was a terrible roar, and all the white faces of the people went even whiter, and they started rushing around, throwing water all over the place as if they were mad.

'What on earth's going on?' asked Nicobobinus.

'We're doomed!' screamed a man.

'Nicobobinus!' yelled Rosie. 'Come here!'

Rosie was standing near the archway that led down to the furnaces. Flames were shooting out more violently than

before. As Nicobobinus reached Rosie's side, a man with a scorched face came racing past.

'It's too late!' he cried. 'It's going to go!'

'More water!' yelled an old man, and the wretched people started rushing about faster than ever.

But Rosie and Nicobobinus took not a bit of notice. They were standing there transfixed, looking at the furnace.

'Am I dreaming?' Nicobobinus asked, 'or is that furnace what I think it is?'

'Nicobobinus!' said Rosie, 'I think I see why the Dwarf-Jester suggested we came here.'

'So do I!' said Nicobobinus.

And the reason Nicobobinus and Rosie both saw what the Dwarf-Jester meant was quite simple. The furnace was a massive affair. It was green and covered in scales, with feet that ended in claws, and a huge mouth filled with sharp teeth from which the flames shot out.

'That furnace,' said Nicobobinus, 'is most definitely a DRAGON!'

23

How Nicobobinus and Rosie Helped a Lot of People But Landed Themselves in Trouble

Before Rosie had time to say 'Journey's End!' or 'I didn't think dragons were as big as *that*!' some of the people started screaming and many of the children began to cry and whimper. And as Nicobobinus and Rosie looked, they began to see the cause for alarm.

The dragon was chained into a great iron stall so that it could not move. Its head was clamped in a sort of iron vice so that its hot firey breath shot through the hole in the wall to heat the cauldrons. It had just room to breathe - which is what Rosie and Nicobobinus had mistaken for the sound of bellows. However it appeared that small flames were actually coming out of the dragon's ears and smoke was billowing out from under its scales.

'This is what always happens!' cried one of the terrified stokers next to Nicobobinus. 'You can keep a dragon chained up like that for a year . . . maybe two years . . . but eventually it burns itself up . . . and everything else as well . . . Oh God! This is it!'

'Well hadn't we all better get out?' yelled Nicobobinus.

The man looked at him and a smile almost crossed his pinched white face.

'That's a good idea,' he said. 'And how do you think we're going to do it? *Eat* our way through the doors? Once they get you down here, they don't let you out again!'

At that moment, the Dragon roared again, and flames seemed to lick out from under its scales for a moment. The wretched people were backing off towards the entrance of the cellar, but they seemed as if mesmerised . . . Their eyes showed no glimmer of hope – like people who had long ago given themselves up to despair, and now watched their fate advancing towards them, devoid of all emotion or desire.

But suddenly Nicobobinus had leapt on the table in the centre of the cellar.

'Run!' he screamed. 'Get out while you still have the *chance*!'

Slowly their eyes turned to him, as if in a dream.

'You *can* get out!' yelled Nicobobinus. 'You're free! Here's the key to this place!' And he lifted up the key to the cellar so that they could all see.

It took several minutes for the information to sink in. These people who had known for so long that they were going to die, could not take in that their release had come.

But then, one by one, a spark of hope leapt into an eye here and an eye there, and then as they looked at each other the spark of hope multiplied, until it burst into a flame and spread through the throng like a forest fire. Nicobobinus threw the key at a girl, whom he recognised as the one who had called for help, when they had first arrived. She caught it, and said: 'I don't know why – but I *knew* you could do it!' Then she rushed to the door, and the rest followed, in a glad panic.

'Come on,' said Rosie, 'let's get out of here!'

'No wait!' cried Nicobobinus, pulling a knife off the wall. 'I'm not leaving here without some dragon's blood!'

Rosie felt, at this moment, that her reputation for having wild ideas was totally unfair.

'But you heard what they said!' she yelled. 'That dragon's going to explode!'

But she might as well have been yelling at the bricks of the cellar walls, for Nicobobinus had disappeared into the furnace room itself.

Rosie took a deep breath, and said to herself:

'If this *were* a story, it wouldn't end like this . . . at least I don't think it would.' And this gave her enough courage to follow Nicobobinus.

The smoke that was seeping out from under the dragon's scales was now black, and the flames shooting out from its jaws and nostrils were almost white hot. It seemed as if the whole of the dragon's body was being consumed by fire from within.

Nicobobinus was standing by the dragon's head, where it lay clamped in the iron vice. The knife was raised in one hand and with the other he was shielding his face from the intense heat.

'Hurry up!' cried Rosie, as flames licked out from the scales on the dragon's belly.

But Nicobobinus just stood there.

'Nico! We've got to get out of here!' cried Rosie. 'Get some blood and let's go!'

But Nicobobinus didn't move. The awful thought suddenly struck Rosie that the dragon's baleful eye, which was fixed on Nicobobinus, might have some magic power to turn him to stone.

'Nico!' she cried. 'Are you all right?' And she rushed

to his side, and as she reached him Nicobobinus lowered the knife.

'I thought it had turned you to stone!' she said.

'No,' said Nicobobinus.

'You're not afraid are you?' said Rosie. 'It can't get at you – look how it's chained.'

'I know,' said Nicobobinus. 'Look at it! Poor thing! Don't you see – it's in pain!'

Rosie looked and saw a great tear roll out of the dragon's baleful eye, that ran down its hot cheek and fizzled up in steam.

Then suddenly the dragon roared again, and the Palace shook, and they saw clearly for the first time the dreadful pain in the dragon's eye.

'It's been chained up here for a year or more, heating King Pactolus's Palace, and now it's burning itself up because it can't move . . .'

'Poor creature!' said Rosie. 'But what can we do?'

'We'll set it free!' cried Nicobobinus. And before Rosie could say: 'That's the second really, truly looney idea you've had in as many minutes,' he was struggling to unfasten the chains that held the dragon's legs.

The heat from the dragon's body was by now so intense that Nicobobinus had to keep retreating. And the iron links of the chain were so hot that he burnt his fingers. Nevertheless, he eventually got it free.

Rosie, meanwhile, was trying to unfasten the vice that clamped the dragon's head. This was even hotter, and she had to get some cloths to bind around her hands before she could turn the great screw that held it tight shut. She could see terrible weals and scars on the dragon's scaly skin, where the iron had dug in, and she wondered to herself how much it must have hurt.

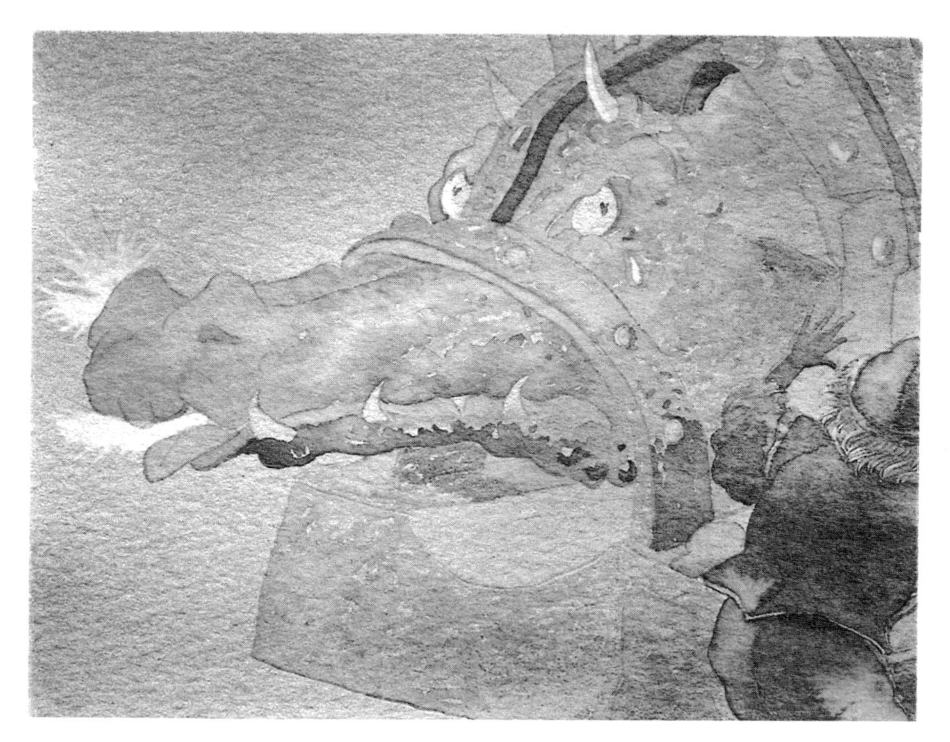

'Fancy being trapped like this for all that time!' she said.

'Look!' cried Nicobobinus. 'It's holding its breath for you!'

And Rosie realised Nicobobinus was right. The dragon was keeping its breath in, so that the flame didn't harm Rosie.

But as it held its breath, it seemed as if all the fire it was keeping inside itself was burning up its body, and the flames began to shoot out from under its scales, and the heat became intolerable.

'I can't turn it any more!' screamed Rosie, and she fell back, shielding her face against the heat.

But Nicobobinus had run in with some wet cloths and with these he was able to give the screw a final turn and the iron mask that had held the dragon's head all that time suddenly sprang back, and the dragon reared up!

Its back arched up against the high ceiling of the cellar,

and its leathery wings beat against the walls and ceiling, and it breathed a great white hot plume of flame, and it roared.

'Run!' yelled Nicobobinus.

And he and Rosie ran as fast as their legs would carry them, back across the great cellar. They pushed against the first great iron door and it slowly opened. Then they seized the handle of the main door. And here they had a nasty shock . . . somebody had locked it again!

24

A Chapter in Which the Story Does *Not* Come to an End!

'This is it!' cried Rosie. 'This *must* be the ending!'

'But this isn't a story!' yelled Nicobobinus. 'This is actually happening to us – and we *can* do something!'

'But *what*?' cried Rosie.

'This!' cried Nicobobinus, and he dashed back into the cellar.

'Aaaargh!' roared the dragon, rolling around on the floor in agony.

'We've got to put it out!' screamed Nicobobinus, and he grabbed a bucket of water that was standing nearby and threw it over the dragon's back. But the dragon was so huge and the heat now so intense, that a mere bucketful simply evaporated the moment the water hit the dragon's scales. It was like a single raindrop falling on a hot stove.

'Aaaargh!' roared the dragon again and the flame from its mouth shot out across the cellar floor and set fire to a table.

'Aaaargh!' it roared again, and it switched its fiery tail, knocking over buckets and chairs and setting fire to everything it touched.

'It's burning the place down!' cried Rosie. 'Nicobobinus! *Do* something!'

Now if I had found myself locked in a cellar with an exploding dragon going berserk and setting fire to the entire building, I think my mind might have gone blank. I don't know what *you* would have done ... perhaps *you* would have done what Nicobobinus did ... He grabbed an axe and threw it at Rosie.

'Catch!' he said.

'What for?' exclaimed Rosie, dropping the axe and nearly chopping off a toe.

'The cauldrons!' yelled Nicobobinus, as he swarmed up one of the ladders on the frame where the cauldrons stood.

'Got it!' cried Rosie. She didn't say: 'Nicobobinus! You're a genius!' or anything like that, because at that moment the dragon roared, and its tail flicked over her head, and she had to fall to the floor before she too rushed up a ladder and joined Nicobobinus as he smashed his axe into the sides of one of the cauldrons.

The sound of splintering wood and the deafening roars of the dragon and the crackle of flames, as the table and other things burnt more and more fiercely, was suddenly drowned by another sound. It was the sound of an avalanche of water dropping from above as the sides of the two cauldrons burst open simultaneously, and the water poured out over the dragon, over the tables, over everything! The cascade almost took Nicobobinus with it, because his golden feet prevented him jumping out of the way in time, but he managed to grab a strut of the platform and just saved himself from being washed down on top of the dragon.

Rosie and Nicobobinus looked around at their handiwork. The floor of the cellar had been instantly transformed into a lake, extinguishing all the fires in a twinkling, and the dragon was rolling around in the water, on its back, on its stomach, dipping its tail in and out, and – most important of all – swallowing great gulps of water by the gallonful to put out the fire within.

'Phew!' said Rosie, wiping the sweat from her smoky forehead.

'Phew!' said Nicobobinus, and he toppled off the platform and landed with a splash in the water.

'Come on in!' he yelled up to Rosie. 'The water's lovely and warm!'

But Rosie didn't answer. She screamed. Nicobobinus looked up, and he screamed as well, for the dragon, which now seemed to have recovered itself, had reared up on its back four legs, and grabbed Rosie in its yellow claws.

'You ungrateful monster!' yelled Nicobobinus. And he plunged his knife into the dragon's foot nearest to him. The bright green blood spurted out covering Nicobobinus from head to foot, and the dragon roared and snatched Nicobobinus up in its other claw. Then it charged against the locked door, smashing it into splinters.

'Put us down!' cried Nicobobinus, stabbing the claw that held him again and again, until the blood was flowing over the monster's claw and Nicobobinus equally. But it made not the slightest difference. The dragon climbed the steps back up into King Pactolus's Palace in a couple of strides. It loped through the smoked-filled halls, across the abandoned courtyard, then burst through the Palace gates, spread its wings and soared into the air.

25

A Very Short Chapter in Which Rosie and Nicobobinus Go a Very Long Way

Nicobobinus looked down as they left the City of Cries far below them. He could see King Pactolus's Palace, surrounded by the winding streets of the city, with here and there a burnt-out ruin – as of some other Palace that had been abandoned in times past, just as King Pactolus was abandoning his Palace now. And there was King Pactolus himself, far below, with all his retinue and belongings, hastening as fast as he could away from his burning Palace. And there too they could see the white-faced toilers from the boiler-room running back to their hovels in the narrow streets.

Nicobobinus suddenly realised that he was still stabbing the dragon's claw. At the same time he realised that the last thing he wanted *now* was for the dragon to let go of him. So he dropped his knife and clung onto the dragon's talon.

The dragon, however, appeared to have no intention of dropping either him or Rosie, but what was just as worrying was that the dragon's strength appeared to be failing, and they began to lose height as it beat its leathery wings slower and slower.

'Come on!' shouted Rosie who, to Nicobobinus, seemed remarkably cheerful. 'We've got to get to the Land of Dragons!'

The dragon roared, and flew slowly on towards the rising sun, and Nicobobinus yelled across to Rosie: 'This is all *your* fault!' Then he gave a big grin.

The dragon seemed to be growing weaker and weaker, yet still it flew on and on, until the City of Cries had disappeared beyond the horizon, and all that lay below them was a vast desert valley of dirt and rock.

Nicobobinus looked at his hands that were still covered with green blood. Then he looked down at his feet, and he could see his boots were full of the dragon's blood, and he felt a tingle running through his whole body. But before he could yell across to Rosie again, they both felt the dragon dropping, and they looked down and saw a strange landscape spread out below them, and they knew that *this* was the Land of Dragons!

26

The Land of Dragons

'It isn't at all like I imagined,' yelled Rosie, as the dragon swooped down and landed under a clump of daisies.

'Nor me!' said Nicobobinus. 'That dandelion over there must be at least a hundred feet tall!'

'And look at the *birds*!' cried Rosie, pointing to a row of sparrows who were doing somersaults on the branch of a stinging-nettle. She became so engrossed by their acrobatics that she quite forgot she was still being held in the claw of a huge, fire-breathing, six-legged dragon.

As for Nicobobinus, he was so amazed by the wooden grass and the trees, that were strolling around like the rich young gentlemen of Venice on a Sunday morning, that *he* quite forgot about his hand *and* feet.

Meanwhile, the dragon had gathered up its last remaining strength and begun to wade across a pink river, over a range of very small snow-capped mountains until it came to a rainbow lake. In the middle of the lake floated a strange castle, that was turning round and round with the twisting eddying of the rainbow waters.

The dragon gave a roar, and the most extraordinary thing happened. A thousand eyes suddenly popped up from the surface of the lake. Then Nicobobinus and Rosie saw that the eyes belonged to a thousand leopards who each looked at them with one eye, then opened the other, and then opened their mouths and began to sing. And as they sang they began to swim around and around, forming patterns and shapes, until they finally all came together, and it seemed as if the leopards all melted into one another to form a wide spotted causeway across the rainbow waters to the strange castle that still span slowly round and round in the centre.

The dragon snorted and limped across the causeway. The castle slowed down, and then stopped. A gateway opened, and Rosie and Nicobobinus found themselves being set down in a courtyard of shining blue marble that made you feel you were walking on the sky.

Nothing, however, absolutely nothing they had seen prepared them for what happened next.

The moment the dragon released them, it seemed to give up the ghost. It heaved a great sigh, and rolled over on its side as good as dead. At the same time they heard a shout and looked up to see the figure of a man slowly descending from the sky, clinging to a giant dandelion puffball.

'I don't believe it!' murmured Nicobobinus.

'It isn't possible!' cried Rosie.

But there was no getting away from it. The man landed gently in the courtyard, then turned round and faced them with a broad smile and an outstretched hand.

'Well!' he beamed. 'This is a surprise!'

'Yes, a very unpleasant one!' thought Rosie.

'You're dead!' exclaimed Nicobobinus. And that's what I thought too, but no! There he was, as large as life: it was the despicable Dr Sebastian.

'Ah! My dear friends! How good to see you!' smiled the Doctor.

'You were thrown overboard by the pirate monks!' exclaimed Nicobobinus.

'Ah! I survived in the most extraordinary way,' replied the Doctor. He then told them a story which, quite frankly, neither Nicobobinus nor Rosie believed.

According to Dr Sebastian, when he was thrown overboard by the pirate monks, they had not even bothered to watch him hit the water. Consequently they did not see what happened next. By one of the most remarkable strokes of luck, at the very moment that the Doctor fell a dolphin happened to be swimming past. And by another equally remarkable stroke of luck, Dr Sebastian happened to land right on the dolphin's back.

The moment he landed on its back, the dolphin dived

down beneath the waves, and took him to a submarine world made out of lump sugar . . .

At this moment Rosie interrupted: 'But surely sugar would dissolve in the sea?'

'I know it doesn't sound very probable,' replied the Doctor, 'but this is what actually happened.'

Anyway, in this strange place, according to the Doctor, he was re-educated by the dolphins. They showed him the error of his ways, and convinced him that his greed for gold only brought unhappiness to everyone, including himself. Then they gave him a degree in medicine. After which he was put into a treacle tart, shot up the inside of an erupting volcano, and landed, just now, here in the Land of Dragons.

As I say, neither Rosie nor Nicobobinus believed a single word of the Doctor's story, and this seemed to irk the Doctor considerably.

'I can't see why you find it so hard to believe *my* story,' he said, 'when here you are in a sky-blue castle spinning around on a rainbow-coloured lake full of singing leopards! I'd have thought my story was pretty believable by comparison.'

Nicobobinus and Rosie found it hard to disagree with this line of argument, and, in any case, the Doctor *had* returned from almost certain death, and he *did* indeed seem to be a reformed character, so they decided not to ask too many awkward questions.

In fact they did not have time to ask *any* awkward questions, for at that very moment there was a terrific roar as if all the doors of Hell had just been opened, and dragons appeared from everywhere – from up on the battlements, from holes in the floor, from doorways, from windows and from the tops of towers.

Great, glistening, deep sea-green monsters surrounded them, glaring from one to the other with fiery hatred.

27

The Dragon's Court

Suddenly a voice boomed out: 'The Dragon's Court is now in session!'

And through a great doorway came the most magnificent dragon, with red wings and golden claws, accompanied by a retinue of smaller dragons, each carrying a giant daisy.

'Once ...' said the Great Dragon, spreading his red wings and rearing up on his back legs, 'the human beings and the dragons lived together in peace ...'

All the other dragons formed a sort of chorus and went 'ahhhh!' and then stood there with rather soppy expressions on their faces.

'Human beings,' continued the Great Dragon, 'were kind to dragons ... picked flowers for them ... wrote them poems ... listened to the dragons singing ...'

'Let them lick their ice-creams!' burst out one little dragon.

'Sh!' went all the others fiercely, and the Great Dragon frowned at the young one, and went on:

'And in return the dragons lit fires for the humans,

warmed up hot stones for their feet in the winter . . . did their ironing . . .'

'Very neatly!' intoned the chorus of dragons.

'But what happened?' demanded the Great Dragon. 'What happened to this world of love and caring between dragons and men?'

'Greed!' chorused the dragons.

'Greed!' responded the Great Dragon. 'Whose greed?'

'Their greed!' chanted the other dragons.

'*Their* greed!' concurred the Great Dragon. 'Greed in the humans who wanted hot running water *all* year round, day *and* night . . . Greed in the men who wanted dragons to slave in their smithies, smelting their iron, forging their swords all round the clock – even during choir practice!'

‘Dum-dee, Dum-dee, Dum-dee DAAAH!’ sang the other dragons in excellent counterpoint.

‘And now,’ continued the Great Dragon, ‘the Kings of the City of Cries have bred a race of Dragon-slayers, – warriors who eat only gold, and who come to this beautiful land to ensnare dragons in cruel traps and iron clamps, and then take them back to warm their palaces!’

‘So *that’s* what Pactolus was going to do with you, Nicobobinus!’ exclaimed Rosie. ‘He was going to feed you to his Dragon-slayers!’

‘Dragon-slayers! Torturers! Murderers!’ chanted the dragons, pointing their scaly claws at Nicobobinus, Rosie and Dr Sebastian.

‘But *we’re* not Dragon-slayers!’ cried Rosie.

'All humans are Dragon-slayers!' chanted the dragons.

'You destroyed the beautiful world we knew!' boomed the Great Dragon. 'Instead of living together with dragons, you sought to use us for your own selfish ends, and in so doing you destroyed the land and created the desert that now lies between us. And still you send your Dragon-slayers to trap us and torture us and destroy us – even though in doing so you are destroying yourselves!'

'Death to the humans!' chanted the dragons.

'Torture them first!' cried a crabby old one.

'Roast them!'

'Fry them!'

'Stick their heads in dragons' jelly!'

'Hang on!' exclaimed Rosie, but no-one could hear her above the roaring of the dragons.

'Are they guilty?' boomed the Great Dragon.

'*Very* guilty!' cried the others.

'Then I condemn them to be taken up as high as a dragon can fly,' said the Great Dragon, 'and then dropped into the furthest ocean'.

'Good idea!' cried all the other dragons.

'I'll do it!'

'No me!'

'I fly higher than him!'

'Stop!' cried another voice, that carried above the noise.

The other dragons turned, and there struggling to its feet was the dragon that had brought Rosie and Nicobobinus to the Land of Dragons. It was pale and shrunken beside the other glossy beasts – its scales were charred, and the weals of the iron chains and the clamps had scarred its lacklustre hide, but its eyes glared fierce and true, and its voice rang out strong and kingly.

'Stop!' it cried again.

'What sort of a dragon are *you*?' demanded the Great Dragon. 'You are hardly green and your scales are charred!'

'I am the Dragon Ashkanet,' said the Dragon.

A chorus of 'Ooooh!' went up from the other dragons and they put on what seemed to Rosie and Nicobobinus a very silly expression of mock-astonishment.

'The Dragon Ashkanet is dead!' said the Great Dragon. 'He was captured by men and put to slavery in their furnaces in the City of Cries!'

'I am Ashkanet,' sighed the old Dragon. 'I am the first dragon to escape from the dungeons of men!'

'Ohhhh?' chorused all the dragons, holding up their forelegs in mock surprise.

'I was rescued by these two children, and I have brought them here to show you what I have learnt in the City of Men.'

'What have you learnt in the City of Men?' chanted the dragons, and they all leapt forward in unison and rested their chins on their forepaws.

'I have learnt that there are good and bad amongst the race of men . . .'

'Heresy!' boomed the Great Dragon. 'All men are bad!'

'Hear me out!' commanded Ashkanet. 'There are the brutal men, the cruel men, the frightened and the weak men. But there are also good and brave men, and this boy and this girl have proved it.'

And then the Dragon Ashkanet told the story of how Rosie and Nicobobinus had taken pity on him and released him from the shackles in King Pactolus's Palace.

The other dragons listened, and broke out into spontaneous applause at the end.

'And I will confirm it!' said Dr Sebastian, suddenly stepping forward.

'Ooooh?' went all the dragons, rolling their eyes and waggling their ears. And Dr Sebastian told the story of how he had been hired to cut off Nicobobinus's hand and feet, and how Rosie had come to the rescue, and then how her presence of mind had rescued all of them from the burning ship.

And once again the dragons burst out into spontaneous applause.

'But why should you cut off this boy's hand and feet?' asked the Dragon Ashkanet.

'Because,' said Dr Sebastian, 'they are made of solid gold'.

Now this information had a most unexpected effect upon the dragons. They all suddenly gave a shriek and leapt back, cowering against the walls of the courtyard, shivering and shaking, and yet at the same time glaring at Nicobobinus with undisguised hatred.

Only the Great Dragon and the Dragon Ashkanet maintained their ground – although they were clearly shaken.

'Surely this cannot be true . . .' stammered the Dragon Ashkanet. 'You would not bring gold into the Land of Dragons.'

Then Nicobobinus stood up and said 'It is true that my hand and feet were changed to gold.'

'Traitor! Dragon-slayer!' hissed the other dragons, still cowering against the wall. And even the Great Dragon took a step back. As for the Dragon Ashkanet, he closed his eyes, and murmured: 'So *that* was where my strength was going on the journey here . . .'

'But that is why I have come to the Land of Dragons

– to seek the cure!' cried Nicobobinus.

'Do you not know that the touch of gold destroys us?' asked the Great Dragon. 'Even the sight of it takes away our will to resist. How else could the Dragon-slayers catch us?'

'But I've found the cure already!' said Nicobobinus, and with that he wiped the dragon's blood off his hand.

The moment he did so, a cry went up from the dragons – half angry, half fearful. And Rosie too cried out, and Nicobobinus looked down at his hand, and he saw, to his total and utter dismay, that it was still as solid gold as ever.

28

The Dragon-Slayers

'Keep away!' said the Great Dragon staggering back.

'I don't mean you any harm!' cried Nicobobinus.

'Then cover that gold!' gasped Ashkanet.

Nicobobinus quickly covered up his golden hand, and looked around at the quivering dragons.

'Well I don't think they're going to be dropping *any* of us into the ocean just now!' murmured Dr Sebastian. 'Well done, Nicobobinus!'

But Nicobobinus turned to Rosie, and she read the despair in his eyes.

'Oh! Rosie . . .' he said. 'What on earth am I going to do? The dragon's blood didn't work.'

Rosie was just about to say: 'Cheer up, Nicobobinus, maybe that dragon was too old and ill, or maybe his blood wasn't the right sort, or maybe you were meant to drink it or maybe . . .' But she never managed to say any of these things, because there was a terrible crash, and the mighty doors of the castle shook.

Something like panic swept through the dragons. They looked from one to the other, and each one seemed to have the same words on its fiery breath: 'Dragon-slayers!' they were saying.

Suddenly the great doors shook again, and this time a crack appeared across them. The dragons gibbered. Rosie grabbed Nicobobinus and Dr Sebastian, and dragged them both behind a buttress, and the Doctor shut his eyes and muttered: 'It was so much quieter with the dolphins ...'

At that moment, a shriek went up from all the dragons. There was a crash, and the doors splintered open. The dragons all buried their heads in their paws, as six shining golden warriors burst into the courtyard.

The Dragon-slayers wore golden armour, that glistened in the sun, and they carried golden crossbows loaded with golden bolts. Behind their golden masks all you could see of their faces was the glitter of cold, golden eyes. And from golden head to golden foot, their skin was shining gold.

'They're just like the Golden Man!' whispered Nicobobinus, peeping out from behind the buttress.

'Ahhhhhh!' went all the dragons, and the air was filled with a great rattling as their scales all shook and their knees knocked together.

The six Dragon-slayers sprang up onto walls and battlements and stood there, hard and glittering, with their deadly golden crossbows aimed at the cowering dragons. Then there was a rumbling and scraping, and Rosie and Nicobobinus saw a huge iron contraption on wheels being dragged and pushed through the castle gates by a hundred of King Pactolus's soldiers.

A great trap was lifted at the head of the cage, and then another hundred soldiers appeared with a huge net of chain-mail and a series of chains.

The rattling of the dragons' scales and the knocking of their knees reached a crescendo, and they all started pointing at each other, whimpering: 'He's more fiery than me . . . I'm hardly hot . . . I couldn't even warm a glass of brandy,' and so on.

But the Dragon-slayers waved their crossbows, and the dragons fell silent. Then the soldiers rushed forward, threw the net over one wretched dragon who went 'Ohh! Not *me*!' They then clamped a vice over its jaws so that it squealed with pain, and dragged it off into the iron cage. Then they wheeled the cage out.

As the soldiers retreated, the Dragon-slayers let off their crossbows – apparently for fun – and the lethal golden bolts went deep into six unfortunate dragons, who screamed and writhed and burst into flames and were gone in a matter of seconds.

'The beasts!' yelled Rosie, leaping out from behind the buttress. 'You cowards! You measlies! I'll beat you black and blue!'

But the Dragon-slayers had gone, hacking and breaking up and destroying the leopard causeway as they went.

The dragons were left dismally staring at the remains of their comrades, as if mesmerised by the six golden bolts that still lay amongst the ashes glistening in the sun.

Nicobobinus leapt up, and picked up the golden bolts. They were still hot from the flames, so he balanced them on his golden hand and then threw them into the rainbow lake.

At once the waters of the lake began to boil and spin until they formed a whirling wall of water around the castle, and then slowly a thousand pairs of eyes appeared from the top of the waterwall, and then the leopards' heads emerged, spinning around with the water, and they opened their mouths and began to sing again.

The song was a lament for the passing of dragons, and for the destruction of the beautiful world that the men and the Dragon-slayers had brought with their gold. And the dragons joined in, mournful and low. And Rosie began to cry, and even Dr Sebastian shook his head and wiped away a tear.

But Nicobobinus was thinking. And this is what he was thinking: 'If the golden bolts had such an amazing effect on the rainbow lake . . . what effect might the rainbow lake have had on the golden bolts? And – even more importantly – what effect might it have on my golden hand?'

Rosie suddenly realised what Nicobobinus was thinking of doing, and something told her that something fearful would happen if he did it. But it was too late! Before she could stop him, Nicobobinus had run across to the rainbow waterwall, and thrust his golden hand into it!

29

Describing the Most Amazing and Extraordinary Events in the Whole Book

The rainbow water washed over his arm and it was warm and felt almost dry to his skin. At the same time he felt a tingle in his golden hand, running up his arm and then into his whole body so that he began to tremble and he felt his head throbbing. Something was definitely happening ... but it wasn't at all what he was hoping would happen.

The note of the song suddenly changed. And instead of singing, the leopards began to howl. Then the wall of water whirled up into the air, and formed a rainbow-coloured ship of water that flew through the sky – a ship just like the Black Ship that had brought Rosie and Nicobobinus to the Land of Dragons. It circled around the blue castle and then sailed off in the direction the Dragon-slayers had taken ... over the tiny snowcapped mountains, across the pink river, over the sauntering trees and the wooden grass, and the acrobatic sparrows and the huge wild flowers, until it hung over the retreating Dragon-slayers and the soldiers hauling the dragon cage.

They all looked up and gasped at the billowing mass

of rainbow water in the sky above them. And they stopped in their tracks and began to cower as if they feared that the deluge was about to drop upon them.

But the water did not fall all at once – it changed into the shape of a cloud, and gently sent down a few drops of precious rainbow rain.

And wherever a drop of rainbow rain touched the earth amazing things happened. The first drops caught the wind and landed on the tiny snow-capped mountains, and the mountains immediately started growing until they were the size of normal mountains. The next drops landed upon the wandering trees, which thereupon ceased wandering aimlessly about, and all ran together, as if summoned by a bugle. They then formed themselves into an army and marched in military style towards the Dragon-

slayers. And before the Dragon-slayers could so much as wind up a crossbow, the trees reached their branches down, and each picked up a Dragon-slayer, and, holding him aloft in its boughs, marched right to the very top of the snow-capped mountains.

The next drops of rainbow rain landed on the wooden grass, and that immediately shot up, wherever it was touched, to form a great fence around King Pactolus's soldiers, trapping them like cattle in a pen. Meanwhile the sparrows stopped their acrobatics, and went and picked the locks of the dragon's cage instead, so the dragon escaped with a roar of gratitude and ran back to the blue castle.

All this time the rainbow cloud of water seemed to be swelling, and as it grew larger and larger it drifted over towards the desert valley. There it hung for a moment

getting still bigger and bigger until it suddenly burst, flooding the valley in a flash and turning it there and then into an instant sea.

Rosie thought she heard the trees on the mountain tops shout, but it may have only been in her mind, and then they bent their boughs back and hurled the Dragon-slayers across the beautiful land right into the middle of the rainbow sea, where they sank like stones to be lost for ever.

And as they disappeared under the waves, the thousand leopards leapt out of the rainbow sea, shook the rainbow water from their backs and then, snarling and howling, raced off towards the City of Cries.

While all this was going on, the dragons had been watching in amazement from the battlements of the blue castle. When all was finally calm again, the Great Dragon turned to Nicobobinus and lifted him up in its claw.

'Forty dragon-cheers for Nicobobinus!' he boomed, and the dragons all cheered, and Rosie cheered and Dr Sebastian brought out a flute and played a sea shanty the dolphins had taught him.

But Nicobobinus was looking miserably at his hand, which was still as solid gold as ever, even though the dragons now seemed to have lost their fear of it.

'Ahem!' said the Great Dragon. 'In view of the services that you have rendered to the beautiful land and to the race of Dragons, it gives me great pleasure to pronounce you all three: "Friends of Dragons". And to inform you that you are free to come and go in the Land of Dragons now and forever.'

Dr Sebastian bowed low, and Nicobobinus muttered 'thanks' and the dragons all cheered again. But Rosie looked rather shocked. 'That's no good!' she exclaimed.

'What else do you want,' snapped the Great Dragon,

'... an embroidered tea-towel?'

'It could say: "Thank you for saving us – love from all the Dragons",' said Dragon Ashkanet.

'No!' said Rosie. 'What I meant was this: you may have got rid of the Dragon-slayers, but there are still dragons being tortured and enslaved in the City of Cries, and there are still men, women and children being treated just as cruelly. We must go and rescue them.'

'Ohhh!' quavered the dragons.

'We dare not go to the City of Cries!' said the Great Dragon.

'Do not ask mc to set foot in that place again!' pleaded the Dragon Ashkanet.

'No need,' said Rosie – get us some dandelion puffballs and you can drop us into the City of Cries, just like Dr Sebastian dropped in here.'

The dragons all looked at each other and held a debate in whispers and dragon-talk. Finally the Great Dragon turned back to Rosie and said: 'It *is* an ingenious plan ... And would you promise to release *all* the dragons as well as the humans?'

'Just like we released the Dragon Ashkanet,' replied Rosie.

'Very well,' said the Great Dragon. 'It is agreed.'

'Hooray!' said Rosie. But at that moment Dr Sebastian said: 'Wait! There is still more to be done.'

The Dragons stopped and looked at him, and then turned to each other and said: 'Fancy that!' 'What can it be?' 'Have you any idea?' 'No. Have you?' and so on and so on.

'Listen,' shouted Dr Sebastian. 'I have seen the ways of the world, and if the dolphins taught me anything about greed they taught me this: the Dragon-slayers may have gone, and you may have captured King Pactolus's army, and the leopards may have chased the King and his crew from the City of Cries, but one day that man will return and build a new army and hire new Dragon-slayers, and he and his descendants will come to destroy you again.'

'This is true,' said the Dragon Ashkanet. 'We must destroy King Pactolus and all his court so that the City of Cries never falls into his hands again.'

'We'll burn him up!' cried the dragons.

'We'll pursue him to the ends of the earth!'

'We'll torture *him*!'

'We'll destroy *him* before he destroys *us*!'

And they all began to rattle their scales and stamp their claws and flap their leathery wings, so that the dust from them rose into the air in clouds, and everyone started coughing and sneezing.

But Nicobobinus, who had been sitting all this time staring at his golden hand, suddenly held it up and shouted: 'No! Don't do *that*!'

Dr Sebastian looked at him in surprise, and the dragons all went: 'Well we never!' 'What's up with *him*?' and so on.

'Surely you're not going to take King Pactolus's part after what he tried to do to you?' whispered Rosie.

Nicobobinus leapt onto a wall, and faced the dragons and Rosie and Dr Sebastian, and said: 'If I have learnt anything from this whole adventure it's this: exactly as the Dragon Ashkanet said, men are just men - there are good and there are bad. Sometimes it is the poor who are evil - like the sailors who first kidnapped me - often it is the rich - like the Golden Man. Sometimes men change - like Dr Sebastian. But this I have seen with my own two eyes: that the ones who seek power over their fellows - like the

Abbot over the pirate monks or King Pactolus over the City of Cries – are almost always all of them bad.

'If we destroy King Pactolus utterly, and every single member of his court, it will make not a scrap of difference. For there will always be someone else to take his place, and others who will help. Some pale-faced wretch who even now toils in the furnaces in the City of Cries, will find such ambition in his soul that he will make himself King and treat the rest just as cruelly as King Pactolus did. And he will make new Dragon-slayers to seek you out and destroy you, just as King Pactolus did.'

'Then what are we to do?' moaned the Dragons. 'Nothing can change.'

'Yes it can!' cried Nicobobinus. 'Leave King Pactolus alone – men are just men. But the City of Cries itself . . . with all its beautiful palaces and graceful streets, with all its furnaces and hovels – *that* you should burn to a cinder!'

There was a silence over all the Dragons and neither Rosie nor Dr Sebastian said anything.

Finally the Great Dragon stood on its back legs, spread its leathery wings and boomed: 'Let's do it!'

30

The Dragons Attack

Rosie climbed onto the Dragon Ashkanet, Nicobobinus climbed onto the Great Dragon, and Dr Sebastian climbed onto a third (whose name was Cynthia). Each of them was holding a giant dandelion puffball, as the air began to vibrate with a beating of leathery wings.

One by one the dragons rose straight up, until they almost blotted out the sun, so thick was the air with dragons of all shapes and sizes.

Slowly they flew over the snow-capped mountains, over the rainbow sea, until they came to the City of Cries, lying under its blanket of snow.

'Here we go!' cried Rosie, and she leapt off the back of Ashkanet, clinging to her puffball, and floated gently down towards the City of Cries. Nicobobinus and Dr Sebastian followed suit, while the dragons wheeled about and circled in the sky.

The City was quite deserted. It seemed as if the leopards had indeed chased off all the inhabitants, for their paw marks mingled with human footprints in the snow that covered the City.

So Nicobobinus, Rosie and Dr Sebastian ran from palace to palace, opening up the cellar doors and releasing the wretched toilers and the dragons alike from the boiler rooms.

'Quick!' they cried. 'Leave the City! The dragons have come! They're going to burn the City to cinders!'

And everyone – women clutching babies, old men on crutches, children and young men, girls and boys – all took one glance above them at the sky dark with dragons, and ran as fast as their legs could carry them, out of the City of Cries.

In the last palace, Nicobobinus found the gates locked. So he hammered on them and cried: 'Come out! The Dragons are here! They've come to burn the City of Cries to a cinder!' And a window opened in the tower above his head and a frightened man looked out.

'Who dares to make such noise in the City of Silence?' he cried.

Nicobobinus looked up and stared. It was King Pactolus himself.

'Oh, it's you!' said King Pactolus. 'Where have you been?'

'They're going to destroy the City!' cried Nicobobinus anxiously, for he could see the dragons above were getting impatient, and were starting to breathe great plumes of flame in the direction of the buildings.

'Did you set those leopards on me?' demanded King Pactolus.

'It doesn't matter!' yelled Nicobobinus. 'You must hurry!'

'I'll be revenged!' cried the King. 'Just you wait!'

'They'll burn you alive if you don't go!' cried Nicobobinus.

'Wait till I get my soldiers back!' cried the king. 'I'll have them slice you limb from limb!'

'Look out!' cried Nicobobinus. But it was too late – a plume of flame suddenly shot down from the sky and engulfed the tower in which King Pactolus was hiding.

'Arrgh!' cried King Pactolus, and dived through the flames onto the pavement below with a terrible crunch.

At that very moment the Palace gates burst open, and out charged the boiler-room toilers, followed by Rosie and Dr Sebastian riding a dragon.

'We got in through a window!' Rosie yelled, as Nicobobinus climbed onto the dragon's back and they all raced out of the City.

Now the dragons began to swoop in, wave after wave, breathing fire in white-hot plumes, until the whole City

became a roaring inferno, and they could feel the heat of it on their backs as they fled.

The dragon on which Rosie, Nicobobinus and Dr Sebastian were riding didn't stop until it reached the shores of the Rainbow Sea. There the other dragons had gathered, standing on tiptoe on boulders to catch their last glimpse of the City burning.

Mingled amongst the dragons were the wan-faced citizens who had escaped from the City of Cries. And as the last palace collapsed in a charred heap the dragons gave forty dragon-cheers, and by the time they got to the fourth, they noticed that the children had joined in. And by the time they got to the fourteenth the adults were cheering, and soon everybody - Man and Dragon - was hugging everybody else and cheering and weeping with joy.

Then Ashkanet the Dragon came up to Nicobobinus and Rosie and said: 'I want to thank you, from the bottom of my dragon's heart, for rescuing not only me, but all of us!'

And the Great Dragon gave them each a medal, and a special medical certificate to Dr Sebastian, and said: 'Is there any gift we can give you?'

Rosie lifted Nicobobinus's golden hand up above him and said: 'We both came to the Land of Dragons to seek a cure for Nicobobinus's golden hand, because we were told that only dragon's blood would cure it. But it didn't seem to. He got Ashkanet's blood all over his hand, but it's still as solid gold as ever.'

'Perhaps he needed to drink it,' said old Ashkanet, and before anyone could stop him the dragon plunged a talon into his own flesh and the bright green blood spurted forth, and Dr Sebastian caught it in a silver cup.

The green blood lay in the silver goblet like liquid emeralds, glinting and sparkling in the evening sun.

Nicobobinus looked around at the smiling faces of the Men and Dragons and took the cup.

'Thank you, Ashkanet,' he said. 'Thank you all. I hope that *none* of us ever has to suffer the curse of gold again.' And so saying, he put the silver cup to his lips and drank down the still-warm, green, dragon's blood. He felt it stinging his lips, and burning his throat, and then he felt it catching fire in his stomach, and the fire coursed through his veins and his golden hand began to throb, and his right foot began to throb, and then his left foot began to throb, and he felt the fire suddenly flash through his body and touch his mind.

Everything went black, and when he came round, he found the Dragon Ashkanet, and Rosie and Dr Sebastian and all the rest gazing anxiously down at him.

'My poor child,' said the Dragon Ashkanet. 'I had no idea my blood would affect you like that.'

'I'm all right!' said Nicobobinus, struggling to his feet. 'I don't care what happens, if I'm cured . . .'

And he held up his hand . . . the hand that had been golden for so long and through so many adventures, and he shut his eyes . . . he could hardly believe it . . . It was still as solid gold as ever!

31

How Rosie and Nicobobinus Returned Home

But before Nicobobinus had a chance to say anything on the lines of 'Bother!', 'Oh dear, what a pity!' or anything that reflected what he *really* felt, he heard the leopards singing behind him. They all turned, and there were the leopards' heads bobbing up and down on the waves of the rainbow sea.

They were singing a song of happiness – that Men and Dragons were together again. And as they sang, a shape rose up out of the rainbow waters. At first neither Nicobobinus nor Rosie recognised what it was, for it was all the colours of the rainbow and more – every plank, every nail, every sheet, and every cleat, every rail and every porthole, every rung and every sail was a different colour. But as it turned towards them, and lowered a rope ladder over the side, there was no mistaking ... It was the Black Ship that had brought them there.

'Stay with us,' said the Great Dragon.

'Stay here,' said Ashkanet.

'Why not?' said Dr Sebastian.

'No,' said Rosie. 'Nicobobinus still isn't cured. If

dragon's blood isn't the answer, we must go back and find out what is.'

And so, despite the pressing of the dragons and the arguments of the townsfolk, Nicobobinus, Rosie and the reformed Dr Sebastian found themselves back on board the Black Ship, sailing off over the Rainbow Sea, around the Ocean of Mountains and out into the wide ocean beyond. There the ship turned slowly towards the east and sailed away from the setting sun.

They were rather surprised, however, to find that they were no longer the only people on board. The ship had acquired a Captain – or at least a man who *claimed* to be the Captain. He was very oddly dressed. He wore a very short skirt which I suppose *we* would nowadays call a *tu-tu*, but which in those days simply didn't exist, a diamond crown and a fisherman's jersey which had, embroidered on the front, 'I love oysters'.

He had absolutely no idea of how he came to be on the Rainbow Boat rising out of the Rainbow Sea, but he was convinced that he was Captain of it, and he showed them all the Captain's log, the Master's log, and the ship's certificate, all of which bore his name – and they knew it was his name because the same name was tattooed in large letters right across his bottom. The name was – Basilcat.

Neither Rosie nor Nicobobinus nor Dr Sebastian really believed Basilcat was captain of anything – let alone the Black Ship. But lacking any other explanation they decided it was just another of those little mysteries of which our lives are full.

The voyage home was uneventful and pleasant. The Ship looked after them, day and night, and both Dr Sebastian and the mysterious Basilcat proved to be honest, reliable and extremely entertaining companions.

‘I think once I may have been a pirate,’ said Basilcat, but he wasn’t really very sure, even though he had a fund of stories to tell about villainy on the high seas – some of them rather rude.

And so they would eat and drink and tell stories of their adventures while the ship sailed steadily homewards.

Nicobobinus, however, remained gloomy and restless, and nothing Rosie did could cheer him up.

They sailed into the Mediterranean, up into the Adriatic Sea. They passed the Land of the Uskoks and they saw the very cliff from which Nicobobinus had been suspended in the cage being gnawed by rats. Then north they sailed, until at last they saw the Venetian lagoon waiting ahead of them.

The Rainbow Ship sailed surely and gracefully through the hidden channels of the lagoon, past Chiogga,

Pellastrina and Malamocco, until at last it arrived in the Basin of San Marco, and cast its anchor within sight of the Doge's Palace.

Basilcat helped them launch a dinghy to carry them ashore, and the Doctor insisted on seeing them both safely home.

As they walked along the familiar canals and narrow streets of Venice, Nicobobinus was downcast. His heavy golden feet echoed wearily amongst the tall buildings. And when they passed the very orchard wall of the Golden Man's house, where it had all begun, it was all Rosie and Dr Sebastian could do to stop Nicobobinus climbing over to find the man who had told him about dragon's blood. 'I'll give him "Dragon's blood"!' growled Nicobobinus.

'Wait until tomorrow,' said Rosie. 'Let's get home now we're here.'

And so they at long last turned across their own little piazza and into their own narrow street and found themselves outside Nicobobinus's door.

'Well, I suppose we'd better say goodbye,' said Dr Sebastian.

'Yes,' said Nicobobinus, sitting gloomily amongst the weeds on the step.

'See you again?' said the Doctor.

'If I haven't been stolen before the morning,' said Nicobobinus miserably.

'Cheer up,' said Rosie. 'We'll find the cure.'

'Yes,' said Dr Sebastian, and then suddenly he gave a bellow. It was so loud that everybody in the street woke up, lit their candles and stuck their heads out of the windows.

'Look! It's Nicobobinus!' they all said.

'Where have you been?!'

'Your Dad's been looking for you high and low!'

'I'm such a fool!' cried Dr Sebastian.

'What's the matter?' asked Rosie.

'I'm forgetting all my medicine – all my knowledge of herbs!'

'What do you mean?' asked Nicobobinus.

'You see that small tree, growing on your doorstep?' said Dr Sebastian.

'Yes,' said Nicobobinus gloomily, 'we never *did* weed that doorstep . . .'

'Lucky you *didn't*!' exclaimed the Doctor. 'That's *Dracaena Draco*!'

'*Dracaena Draco*?' said Rosie, pulling a face. 'What's that?'

'That's its Latin name, but everyone usually calls it a Dragon Tree. And if you cut it, you get . . .'

'*DRAGON'S BLOOD*!' shouted Rosie, Nicobobinus and Dr Sebastian all together.

In a twinkling, Nicobobinus had made a cut in the tree. A dark red resin oozed out, and in no time Nicobobinus had rubbed some of it onto his golden hand and his golden feet and his golden neck. Wherever the Dragon's Blood touched his golden skin, he felt a tingle. Then he felt the life rushing back into his body, as the gold began to lose its lustre, and finally turned back into flesh and blood.

'Nicobobinus! What on earth are you doing, dancing around in the street at this time of night?' called Nicobobinus's father.

'And where have you been?' called his mother, in her night cap.

'I've just sailed half-way round the world to find some Dragon's Blood!' laughed Nicobobinus. 'And here it was all the time growing on my own doorstep!' and he did cartwheels and somersaults and handstands and handsprings – he was so glad to be his old self again.

The neighbours tut-tutted and shut their shutters. And then Nicobobinus and Rosie and Dr Sebastian went inside and told their stories to their families over mugs of warm milk and hunks of bread and cheese – although, I have to tell you, there were many parts of the story that nobody believed.

And that's really all there is to tell about what happened when Rosie said: 'Let's discover the Land of Dragons.' As far as Rosie was concerned it all went to prove that her friend really could do anything . . . but then, come to think of it, so could she.

'But hold on a minute!' you may be saying. 'At the

start you said that Nicobobinus was the most extraordinary child who ever stuck his tongue out at the Prime Minister.'

Well, yes ... I admit I *did* say that, and I'm afraid I just made it up. I also have to admit to you that I made it up about not knowing what happened to Basilcat. I *do* know, but then I don't see why that should worry you. After all I made it up about the Black Ship, I made it up about the Dragons, I made it up about Rosie. I made it up about Nicobobinus. In fact ... to tell you the honest truth ... I even made it up about myself. Because you see I *was* Basilcat ... But then that's another story too ...